Judith Hermann

was born in 1970, and lives in Berlin. *The Summer House, Later* is her first book.

From the international reviews for *The Summer House, Later*:

'This debut from a young German writer has created quite a stir in her home country. *The Summer House, Later* is an exquisite and powerful collection of melancholic snapshots of everyday life. The ghosts of Carver and Chekhov stalk the pages, and Hermann's precise use of language, unstinting lack of bathos and cool, glacial tones are often spellbinding. Through her economic use of words, the author succeeds in drawing the reader irrevocably into each of the nine stories.'
Scotland on Sunday

'The fragility of life's decisions are relayed without sentimentality, yet with a quiet melancholy. An exceptional debut that gives rise to great hope.'
Die Zeit

'A book about a certain kind of young woman, trying to get a boyfriend, to get some fun out of life, but with a sense of melancholy, a sense of loneliness, that seems to define a generation.'
Publishers Weekly

'A bittersweet collection that manages to capture perfectly the feeling of just-out-of-reach satisfaction. Margot Bettauer Dembo's sensitive translation means that Hermann's prose remains as clear and measured as it is in the original German.'
Sunday Tribune (Dublin)

'One of the great revelations of contemporary German literature . . . Hermann knows exactly how to choose the right details, and makes her music with   the reader is held by it still and rega   *Monde*

overleaf

'With her first short story collection, Judith Hermann reveals herself to be a remarkable writer with a sure grasp of her craft and an almost overwhelming sense of humanity. Her stories, principally set in the peeling city of Berlin, are elevated above the urban landscape by an elegantly filed prose that captures the world that survives underneath the fingernails of the everyday.' *RTE Guide*

'Exceptional . . . In Hermann's fiction, intricately fashioned worlds reveal themselves, worlds which are utterly absorbing, sometimes heartbreaking, and always starkly original . . . a collection of striking distinction and poise . . . Every story here is worth reading. All of them possess merit and some of them touch on brilliance. When Hermann is on form, she can rival the best contemporary exponents of short fiction.' *Sunday Business Post*

'*The Summer House, Later* has an irresistible power . . . No word is too much and none out of place.' *Neue Zürcher Zeitung*

'Melancholy, muted, sometimes dramatic, but always pointed, precise and without pathos . . . The drama of Judith Hermann's stories comes from what is unsaid, from a tension between artful staging and that which really happens, but is only glimpsed.'
  Tagesspiegel

'Beautifully written, haunting stories . . . The settings range from urban squalor to Costa Rica, but the characters mirror each other's aimlessness, depression and fear. These people are living fractured lives, remembering the past without learning from it, frightened of the future, and unable to engage with the present.' *Tablet*

'An elegant and perceptive reading on the emptiness that fills our lives . . . Judith Hermann is a master storyteller.' *Independent*

JUDITH HERMANN

The Summer House,
Later

Translated from the German by
Margot Bettauer Dembo

Flamingo
An Imprint of HarperCollinsPublishers

Flamingo
An imprint of HarperCollins*Publishers*
77–85 Fulham Palace Road,
Hammersmith, London W6 8JB

Flamingo is a registered trade mark of
HarperCollins*Publishers* Limited

www.**fire**and**water**.com

Published by Flamingo 2002
9 8 7 6 5 4 3 2 1

First published in Great Britain by Flamingo 2001

First published in German by S. Fischer Verlag as *Sommerhaus, Später* 1998

Judith Hermann asserts the moral right to
be identified as the author of this work

Margot Bettauer Dembo asserts the moral right to
be identified as the translator of this work

These stories are works of fiction. The names,
characters and incidents portrayed in them are the work of the
author's imagination. Any resemblance to actual persons,
living or dead, events or localities is entirely coincidental.

Photograph of Judith Hermann © Renate von Mangoldt

Flamingo wishes to thank Andrew Wille for
his copy-editing work on the English edition.

ISBN 0 00 711576 8

Set in Minion

Printed and bound in Great Britain by
Clays Ltd, St Ives plc

For F.M. and M.M.

Contents

The doctor says, I'll be alright
but I'm feeling blue

Tom Waits

The Red Coral Bracelet

My first and only visit to a therapist cost me my red coral bracelet and my lover.

The red coral bracelet came from Russia. To be more precise, it came from St Petersburg and was more than a hundred years old. My great-grandmother had worn it on her left wrist; it cost my great-grandfather his life. Is that the story I want to tell? I'm not sure. Not really sure—

My great-grandmother was beautiful. She went to Russia with my great-grandfather because my great-grandfather was building furnaces there for the Russian people. My great-grandfather rented a large apartment for my great-grandmother on Vasilevsky Ostrov, one of the islands of St Petersburg. The Greater and the Lesser Neva lapped at the shores of Vasilevsky Ostrov, and if my great-grandmother had stood on tiptoe to look out of the window in her apartment on Maly Prospekt she would have seen the river and the great Kronstadt Bay. But my great-grandmother did not want to see the river or Kronstadt Bay or the beautiful tall houses on Maly Prospekt. She did not want to look out of the window at a foreign land. She drew the heavy red velvet drapes and shut the doors – the carpets swallowed all sound, and my great-grandmother sat on the sofas, the chairs, or the four-poster beds, rocking back and forth and feeling homesick for Germany. The light in the large apartment on Maly Prospekt was dim, like the light at the bottom of the sea, and my great-grandmother may have thought that this foreign place, that St Petersburg, that all of Russia was nothing but a deep, twilight dream from which she would soon awaken.

My great-grandfather, though, was travelling all over the country building furnaces for the Russian people. He built shaft furnaces and roasting kilns and self-dumping reverberatory furnaces and Livermore furnaces. He stayed away for a long time. He wrote letters to my great-grandmother, and whenever one of these letters arrived my great-grandmother would open the heavy red drapes a little and read by the narrow chink of daylight:

> *I would like to explain to you that the Hasenclever furnace we are building here consists of muffles that are connected to each other by vertical channels and are heated by the flames of a grate-firing furnace – you remember, don't you, the retort furnace I built in the Blome Wildnis in Holstein, which you liked so much at the time? Well, in the Hasenclever furnace the ore is also loaded through an opening in the top muffle and . . .*

Reading these letters made my great-grandmother very weary. She could no longer remember the retort furnace in the Blome Wildnis but she could remember the Blome Wildnis, the pastures and the flat countryside, the hay bales in the fields and the taste of cold, sweet apple cider in the summer. She let the room subside once more into its twilight and lay down wearily on one of the sofas, repeating, 'Blome Wildnis, Blome Wildnis.' It sounded like a children's song, like a lullaby, it sounded nice.

In those years, in addition to foreign businessmen and their families, many Russian artists and scholars lived on Vasilevsky

Ostrov. It was inevitable that they would hear of the German woman, the beautiful pale one with the fair hair who was said to live up on Maly Prospekt, almost always by herself and in rooms as dark, soft and cool as the sea. The artists and scholars went to see her. My great-grandmother gestured with her small weary hand, asking them to come in. She spoke little, she scarcely understood anything they said, slowly and dreamily she gazed at them from under heavy eyelids. The artists and scholars sat down on the deep, soft sofas and chairs, sinking into the heavy, dark materials; the maids brought black cinnamoned tea with huckleberry and blackberry jam. My great-grandmother warmed her cold hands on the samovar and felt much too tired to ask the artists and scholars to leave. And so they stayed. And they looked at my great-grandmother, and in the dusk my great-grandmother merged into something melancholy, beautiful and foreign. And since melancholy and beauty and foreignness are essential traits of the Russian soul, the artists and scholars fell in love with my great-grandmother, and my great-grandmother let herself be loved by them.

My great-grandfather stayed away for a long time. And so my great-grandmother let herself be loved for a long time – she did it carefully and circumspectly, and she made hardly any mistakes. Warming her cold hands on the samovar and her chilled soul on the ardent hearts of her lovers, she learned to distinguish – in that strange, soft language of theirs – the words: 'You are the most tender of all birches.' She read the letters about the smelting furnaces, the Deville furnaces and the tube furnaces in the narrow chink of daylight and burned them all in the fireplace. She allowed herself to be loved; in the evening before falling asleep she sang the song about the Blome Wildnis, sang it to herself, and when her lovers looked at her inquiringly, she smiled and said nothing.

*   *   *

My great-grandfather promised to come back soon, to take her back to Germany soon. But he did not come.

The first, the second, and then the third St Petersburg winter passed, and still my great-grandfather was busy building furnaces in the Russian vastness, and still my great-grandmother was waiting for the day when she could return home to Germany. She wrote to him in the taiga. He replied that he would come back soon but that he would have to leave again one more time, just one last time – but then, but then, he promised, then they could leave.

The evening of his arrival my great-grandmother was sitting in front of the mirror in her bedroom, combing her fair hair. The gifts from her lovers lay in a little jewellery box before the mirror: the brooch from Grigori, the ring from Nikita, the pearls and velvet ribbons from Alexei, the locks of hair from Jemelyan, the medallions, amulets and silver bracelets from Mikhail and Ilya. The little jewellery box also held the red coral bracelet from Nikolai Sergeyevich. Its six hundred and seventy-five little coral beads were strung onto a silken thread, and they glowed as red as rage. My great-grandmother put the hairbrush down in her lap, and closed her eyes for a long time. Then she opened her eyes again, took the red coral bracelet from the little box and fastened it around her left wrist. Her skin was very white.

That evening, for the first time in three years, she shared a meal with my great-grandfather. My great-grandfather spoke Russian and smiled at my great-grandmother. My great-grandmother folded her hands in her lap and smiled back at him. My great-grandfather talked about the steppes, about the wilderness, about the Russian 'White Nights', he talked about the furnaces and called them by their German names, and my great-grandmother nodded as though she understood. My great-grandfather told her in Russian that he had to go once more to Vladivostok, eating pelmeni with his fingers as he said it; he wiped the grease from his lips with his hands. He said that Vladivostok was his last stop, then it would be time to return to Germany. Or would she like to stay longer?

My great-grandmother did not understand what he said, but she recognized the word Vladivostok. She placed her hands on the table, and on her white left wrist the coral bracelet glowed red as rage.

My great-grandfather stared at the coral bracelet. He put what was left of his pelmeni back on his plate, wiped his hands on the linen napkin, and gestured to the maid to leave the room. In German, he said, 'What's that?'

My great-grandmother said, 'A bracelet.'

My great-grandfather said, 'And where did you get it, if I may ask?'

Very softly and gently my great-grandmother said, 'You may. I wish you had asked me all along. It's a present from Nikolai Sergeyevich.'

My great-grandfather called the maid back and sent her to get his friend Isaak Baruw. Isaak Baruw arrived; he was hunchbacked and stooped, and he looked sleepy and confused, it was already late at night and he kept running his fingers through his uncombed hair, embarrassed. My great-grandfather and Isaak Baruw walked around the room, agitated and arguing; in vain Isaak Baruw spoke calming words, words that reminded my great-grandmother of her lovers. Exhausted, my great-grandmother sank into one of the soft easy chairs and put her cold hands on the samovar.

My great-grandfather and Isaak Baruw were speaking Russian, and my great-grandmother didn't understand much more than the words 'second' and 'Petrovsky Park'. The maid was handed a letter and sent out into the dark. At dawn my great-grandfather and Isaak Baruw left the house. My great-grandmother had fallen asleep in the soft easy chair, her small hand and wrist with the red coral bracelet hanging limply from the arm of the chair. It was as dark and still in the room as the bottom of the sea.

Towards noon Isaak Baruw came back and, amidst much bowing and scraping and many condolences, informed my great-grandmother that my great-grandfather had died at eight o'clock that morning. On the hill in Petrovsky Park, Nikolai Sergeyevich had shot him straight through the heart.

My great-grandmother waited seven months. Then, on 20 January in the year 1905, during the first days of the revolution, she gave birth to my grandmother, packed her suitcases, and returned to Germany. The train to Berlin turned out to be the last one to leave St Petersburg before the railroad workers went on strike and all traffic between Russia and the outside world was halted. As the doors of the train closed and the locomotive blew white steam into the winter air there appeared at the far end of the platform the crooked, hunchbacked figure of Isaak Baruw. My great-grandmother saw him coming and ordered the conductor to wait, so at the last second Isaak Baruw climbed aboard. He accompanied my great-grandmother on the long journey to Berlin, carrying her suitcases and hatboxes and handbags, and he did not miss a chance to assure her repeatedly of his lifelong gratitude. My great-grandmother smiled at him comfortingly but did not speak. She was wearing the red coral bracelet on her left wrist, and even then my tiny grandmother in the willow basket already bore more of a resemblance to Nikolai Sergeyevich than to my great-grandfather.

My first and only visit to a therapist cost me the red coral bracelet and my lover.

My lover was ten years older than I, and he looked like a fish. He had fish-grey eyes and fish-grey skin, and, like a dead fish, lay on his bed all day long, cold and silent; he was in a very bad way, lying around on his bed, and when he said anything at all said only a single sentence: 'I am not interested in myself.' Is that the story I want to tell?

I don't know. I don't know really—

My lover was Isaak Baruw's great-grandson, and in his thin veins ran Russian-German blood. Isaak Baruw had remained true to my great-grandmother all his life, but it was her Pomeranian chamber-maid that he married. He fathered seven children with her, and these seven children presented him with seven grandchildren, and one of these grandchildren presented him with his only great-grandson – my lover. My lover's parents drowned in a lake during a summer storm, and my great-grandmother ordered me to go to the funeral – the last witnesses of her St Petersburg past were being lowered into the soil of Brandenburg and with them went the stories she herself no longer wanted to tell. And so I went to the funeral of Isaak Baruw's grandson and his wife, and my lover stood at their grave and wept three grey tears. I took his cold hand in mine, and when he went home I went with him; I thought I could console him with the St Petersburg stories; I thought that he could then tell them to me as though they were new.

But my lover did not speak. And he didn't want to listen to anything, and he knew nothing of the winter morning in the year

1905 when my great-grandmother kept the train from leaving so that his great-grandfather could escape at the very last moment. My lover just lay on his bed and, when he said anything at all, spoke just this one sentence: 'I am not interested in myself.' His room was cold and dusty and faced the cemetery, where the death bells rang constantly. If I stood on tiptoe and looked out of the window, I could see the freshly dug graves, the bouquets of carnations and the mourners. I would often sit on the floor in a corner of the room, knees drawn up to my chest, gently blowing the dust balls through the room. I thought it strange for someone not to be interested in himself. I was interested exclusively in myself. I looked at my lover, and my lover looked at his body as if it were already dead; sometimes we would make love like enemies, and I would bite his salty mouth. I felt slender and skinny, even though I wasn't; I could act as though I were not myself. The light coming through the trees outside the window was green, a watery light, a light one sees near lakes, and fluffs of dust floated through the room like algae and seaweed.

My lover was sad. Sympathetically I asked him whether I should tell him a short Russian story and my lover replied enigmatically that the stories were over, he didn't want to hear them, and anyway I wasn't to confuse my own story with other stories. I asked him, 'And do you have a story of your own?' and my lover said, no he had none. But twice a week he went to a doctor, a therapist. He forbade me to go with him; he refused to tell me anything about the therapist, and said, 'I talk about myself. That's all.' And when I asked him whether he talked about the fact that he wasn't interested in himself he looked at me with contempt and said nothing.

*   *   *

So my lover was either silent or he repeated his single sentence. I was silent, too, and I began to think about the therapist, my face always as dusty as the soles of my bare feet. I imagined myself sitting in the therapist's office, talking about myself. I had no idea what I should talk about. I hadn't really talked for a long time; for as long as I had been with my lover I hardly spoke with him, and he practically never talked with me, saying only this one sentence. There were times when I thought the language consisted solely and exclusively of six words: 'I am not interested in myself.'

I began to think a lot about the therapist. I thought only of talking to him in an unfamiliar room, and that was pleasant. I was twenty years old, and I had nothing to do, and on my left wrist I wore the red coral bracelet. I knew the story of my great-grandmother; in my mind I could walk through the dark, twilight apartment on Maly Prospekt, and I had seen Nikolai Sergeyevich in my grandmother's eyes. The past was so tightly intertwined within me that it sometimes seemed like my own life. The story of my great-grandmother was my own story. But where was my story without my great-grandmother? I didn't know.

The days were silent, as though under water. I sat in my lover's room, and the dust wove itself around my ankles. I sat, knees drawn up to my chest, my head on my knees, and with my index finger I would draw symbols on the grey floor; I was lost in thought about I don't know what. It seemed years passed this way; I was just drifting along. Could I talk about it? From time to time my great-grandmother came by and with a bony hand knocked on the apartment door, calling for me to come out and go home with her, her voice sounding as if it came from a great distance through the dust that had spun about the door. I made no move and did not answer her, my lover also just lay on his bed without moving and stared at the ceiling with dead eyes. My great-grandmother called to me, luring me with pet names from my childhood – dear heart, little nut tree, precious heart – insistently and doggedly she tapped with her bony hand on the door. Only when I called out triumphantly, 'You sent me to him, now you have to wait until it's over!' did she finally go.

I heard her footsteps on the stairs getting softer and softer; at the door, the dust balls disturbed by her knocking settled and gathered into a thick mass of fluff. I looked at my lover and said, 'Are you sure you wouldn't like to hear the story about the red coral bracelet?'

Lying on the bed my lover turned toward me with a tortured face. He stretched out his fish-grey hands and slowly spread his fingers, his fish-grey eyes protruding slightly from their sockets. The silence of the room quivered like the surface of a lake into which one has thrown a stone. I showed my lover my arm and the red coral beads on my wrist, and my lover said, 'Those are members of the family Coralliidae. They form a little stem that can grow to be three feet tall, and they have a red, horny skeleton of calcium. Calcium.'

My lover spoke with a lisp, awkwardly and slurring his words as though he were drunk. 'They grow off the coast of Sardinia and Sicily, Tripoli, Tunis, and Algeria. There, where the sea is as blue as turquoise, very deep, one can swim and dive, and the water is warm . . .' He turned away from me again and sighed deeply; he kicked the wall twice then he lay still.

I said, 'Listen, I want to tell you the stories! The St Petersburg stories, the old stories. I want to tell them so I can leave them all behind and move on.'

My lover said, 'I don't want to hear them.'

I said, 'Then I'll tell them to your therapist,' and my lover sat up, taking a deep breath so that several fluffs of dust disappeared in a small stream into his gaping mouth, and said, 'You're not going to tell my therapist anything, you can go to anyone else, but not to my therapist.' He coughed and thumped his naked grey chest, and I had to laugh because my lover had never before talked so much at one stretch. He said, 'You're not going to talk about me with someone to whom I talk about myself, that's impossible,' and I replied, 'I don't want to talk about you, I want to tell the story; and my story is your story too.' We were really fighting with each other. My lover threatened to leave me; he grabbed me and pulled my hair, he bit my hand and scratched me, a wind blew through the room, the windows flew open, the death bells in the cemetery rang like crazy, and the dust balls drifted out like soap bubbles. I pushed my lover away and ripped the door open; I really felt thin and skinny. As I was leaving I could hear the dust balls sinking softly to the floor, my lover with his fish-grey eyes and his fish-grey skin standing silent next to his bed.

The therapist, whose fault it was that I lost my red coral bracelet and my lover, was sitting in a large room behind a desk. The room was really very large, almost empty except for this desk, the therapist behind it, and a little chair in front of it. A soft, sea blue, deep blue carpet covered the floor. As I entered the therapist looked at me solemnly, looked me straight in the eye. I walked towards him. I had the feeling of having to walk for a very long time before I finally reached the chair in front of his desk. I thought about the fact that my lover usually sat on this chair and spoke about himself – about what? – and felt a tiny sadness. I sat down. The therapist nodded at me. I nodded too and stared at him, waiting for it to begin, for the conversation to start, for his first question. The therapist stared back at me until I lowered my eyes, but he said nothing. He was silent. His silence reminded me of something. It was very quiet. Somewhere a clock I couldn't see was ticking: the wind blew around the tall house. I looked at the sea blue, deep blue carpet beneath my feet and pulled nervously and diffidently at the silk thread of the red coral bracelet. The therapist sighed. I raised my head, and he tapped the gleaming desktop with the needle-sharp point of his pencil. I smiled in embarrassment, and he said, 'What is it that's worrying you?'

I took a breath, raised my hands, and let them drop again. I wanted to say that I wasn't interested in myself, but I thought, That's a lie, I'm interested only in myself, and is that it? That actually there is nothing? Only the weariness and the empty, silent days, a life like that of fish under water and laughter without reason? I wanted to say that I had too many stories inside me, they put a burden on my life; I thought, I could just as well have stayed with my lover; I took a breath, and the therapist opened his mouth and his eyes wide, and I tugged at the silken thread of the red coral bracelet and the silk thread broke and the six hundred and seventy-five red-as-rage little coral beads burst in glittering splendour from my thin, slender wrist.

Distraught, I stared at my wrist; it was white and naked. I stared at the therapist, who was leaning back in his chair, the pencil now in front of him, parallel to the edge of the desk, his hands folded in his lap. I covered my face with my hands. I slipped off the chair onto the sea blue, deep blue carpet; the six hundred and seventy-five coral beads were scattered all over the room. They gleamed, more rage-red than ever before, and I crawled around on the floor and gathered them up. They were lying under the desk, under the therapist's toes, and he drew his foot back a tiny bit as I touched it. It was dark under the desk, but the red coral beads glowed.

I thought of Nikolai Sergeyevich; I thought, if he hadn't given my great-grandmother the red coral beads, if he hadn't shot my great-grandfather in the heart. I thought of the hunchbacked, stooped Isaak Baruw; I thought, if he hadn't left Russia, if my great-grandmother hadn't stopped the train for him. I thought of my lover, the fish; I thought, if he hadn't been silent all the time I wouldn't now have to crawl around under a therapist's desk. I saw the therapist's trouser legs, his folded hands, I could smell him. I bumped my head on the desktop. Once I had collected all the red coral beads under the desk, I crawled back into the light and across the room, picking up the coral beads with my right hand and holding them in my left. I began to cry. I was kneeling on the soft, sea blue, deep blue carpet, looking at the therapist, the therapist looking at me from his chair with his hands folded. My left hand was full of coral beads, but there were more still glowing and blinking all around me. I thought it would take me all my life to pick up all these coral beads, I thought I would never get it done, not during a whole lifetime. I stood up. The therapist leaned forward, picked the pencil up off his desk, and said, 'The session is over for today.'

I poured the red coral beads from my left hand into my right. They made a lovely, tender sound, almost like gentle laughter. I raised my right hand and flung the red coral beads at the therapist. The therapist ducked. The red coral beads rained down onto his desk, and with them all of St Petersburg, the Greater and the Lesser Neva, my great-grandmother, Isaak Baruw and Nikolai Sergeyevich, my grandmother in the willow basket and my lover the fish, the Volga, the Luga, the Narva, the Black Sea, the Caspian Sea and the Aegean Sea, the Gulf of Finland, the Atlantic Ocean.

The waters of the earth's oceans surged in a huge green wave over the therapist's desk and ripped him out of his chair. The water rose rapidly and lifted the desk up with it. Once more the therapist's face emerged from the billows, and then it disappeared. The water roared, broke and sang, swelling and flushing away the stories, the silence and the coral beads, flushing them back into the seaweed forests, into the shell beds, to the bottom of the sea. I took a deep breath.

I went back one last time to see how my lover was doing. He was drifting – I knew he would be – on his watery bed, his pale belly turned to the ceiling. The light was as grey as the light at the bottom of a lake; dust balls were caught in his hair, trembling softly. I said, 'You know that coral turns black when it lies too long at the bottom of the sea.' I said, 'Was that the story I wanted to tell?' But my lover could no longer hear me.

Hurricane
(*Something Farewell*)

The game is called 'Imagining a Life Like That'. You can play it evenings when you're sitting at Brenton's Place on the Island, smoking cigarettes and drinking rum and Coke. It helps to have a little sleeping island child whose hair smells of sand in your lap. The sky should be clear, preferably filled with stars, and it should be very hot, perhaps even humid. The game is called 'Imagining a Life Like That'; it has no rules.

'Just imagine it,' Nora says. 'Just imagine.'

On the radio they're broadcasting hurricane reports four times a day. Kaspar says it doesn't get critical until the hurricane reports come every hour. Then the islanders would be asked to go to special safety zones. German citizens could ask their embassy to arrange for them to be flown to the United States. Kaspar is quite determined, saying, 'I won't leave the Island.' He is going to stay, and he expects all of Stony Hill and Snow Hill will seek shelter at his place. The Island is in the low-pressure region of the tropical depression. Nora and Christine are sitting on the sun-dry wooden boards of the porch, raptly repeating to themselves, 'Tropical depression, tropical . . .'

It is unbearably hot. Thick white clouds motionless above the Blue Mountains. The hurricane, named 'Bertha' by the meteorologists, is building up far away over the Caribbean; it isn't moving but seems to be gathering strength for Cuba, Costa Rica, the Island.

*   *   *

Cat beats Lovey, Nora later writes to Christine, who is already back home in the city, *Cat beats Lovey, and Lovey beats Cat, oh Christine my dear, it's not really your fault. Kaspar talks too much: I like you, I like you; he carves wooden birds, and I only wish he'd leave me alone once in a while; dearest Christine, I miss you . . .* Christine is reading this at the kitchen table, her legs drawn up to her chest. Sand trickles from the pages of the letter. She marvels at how things always have their effect, feels far removed from the Island, feels tired, too.

Kaspar knows that Christine kissed Cat – on her last evening on the Island. They had driven down to Stony Hill in the Jeep. 'Let's drive to Brenton's Place, okay?' Christine had begged, wide-eyed. Kaspar let himself be persuaded. He liked Christine's phrase 'Brenton's Place' to designate Brenton's store, a wooden shack in the village, in the shade of a breadfruit tree; you could drink dark rum there and buy Craven 'A' cigarettes by the piece while old men play dominoes with grim concentration, and a long drawn-out high-pitched whistle comes out of Brenton's radio. They had driven down to Stony Hill in the Jeep, and the clouds had parted to permit a view of the high, star-spangled sky.

Brenton had a new refrigerator. Christine duly admired it, but she was restless and kept staring hard into the darkness towards Cat's bench at the edge of the clearing – 'Is he sitting there or isn't he?'

Kaspar knew very well that Cat was sitting there. Cat always sat there; all the same Kaspar said, 'No idea,' gloating over Christine's anxious indecision. Christine, nervous, quickly drank her dark rum, tugged at Nora's dress, then ran out and was swallowed up by the darkness. After some time her white legs were seen dangling down from the bamboo bench.

'Because he was clicking his cigarette lighter,' she said later, proud of her powers of deduction, and Kaspar remembers the pale shadow of her face, turning towards something and merging with it. Later, when he and Nora wanted to drive home, he called her name. At first she didn't answer, then some minutes later she said, 'Yes?' in a very sleepy and soft voice before jumping up off the bench and silently getting into the Jeep. Kaspar knows that she kissed Cat and made him God-knows-what promises; he does not approve.

But it's Nora and Christine's first time on the Island. Kaspar doesn't miss the chance to repeat this every day: he sings it to himself. After a week of this Nora says firmly, 'Kaspar, enough now.'

'You're always so amazed by every little thing,' Kaspar says. '"Look at those guavas," and "Look at that sunset sky," that's ridiculous too.'

In the hammock Christine yawns sleepily and says, 'Kaspar, you've simply been here too long, you *live* here, that's what makes the difference.' Kaspar, triumphantly, says, 'That's why I have to keep saying it – it's Nora and Christine's first time on the Island.'

Kaspar is no longer amazed. Guavas, mangoes, papayas, lemons big as a child's head. Coconuts, lianas, azaleas. Spiders hopping through the room like frogs, the tiniest salamanders and poisonous millipedes. The fruit of the akee that looks like an apple and when fried tastes like an egg. Mangoes are cut open and then spooned out. 'Are you thirsty?' Kaspar asks graciously, getting a coconut from the garden, cracking it open and pouring the white, milky liquid into glasses. 'Good,' says Nora. She makes a face as if to say there's a first time for everything, then says, 'Kaspar, stop watching me.'

Christine collects everything. Coconut shells, black seashells, akee pits, palm fronds, matches, butterfly wings. 'What are you going to do with that stuff?' Kaspar asks. Christine says, 'Well, it's to show them. Back home.' Kaspar replies, 'They won't be interested.'

Since Nora and Christine arrived Cat has been coming to see Kaspar almost every day. But this isn't really anything new. Cat comes around often; he is a friend of Kaspar's and he helps on the farm. But Kaspar is surprised by the persistence with which Cat – mangoes, papayas, and lemons in his backpack – now takes the steep and rocky road to Kaspar's house every morning in the blazing sun, silently puts the fruit on the kitchen table, then goes to sit down on the porch, only to lapse into immobility. Kaspar watches Cat, who leans back in the blue porch chair, his eyes, as always, half closed, smoking a lot of hashish, clicking his lighter open and shut with his thumb and watching Nora and Christine. They remain unresponsive, noticing nothing; besides it's hot, and they're much too close to each other to be aware of a stranger's attentions. In the morning they drink unsweetened black coffee, smoke five Craven 'A' cigarettes in a row, cadge some coconuts from Kaspar, restless to do something, then run down the meadow and disappear. Kaspar feels shut out and is angry. He would have liked to have more of Nora to himself; after all, that was the reason for her visit. He says 'Back then'. He says 'Remember', he says 'We' and 'We in the city back then', such funny words. Christine raises her eyebrows mockingly and Nora looks away.

'That was then, Kaspar,' she says, kissing him on the cheek. She wants, perhaps, a new kind of friendship, perhaps nothing at all any more.

'Why did you come anyway?' Kaspar asks. Nora answers

casually, 'Because you invited us,' or, 'Because I felt like seeing you. How you live here, and if you've changed.'

'Have I changed?' Kaspar asks himself. 'Did I come here to *change*?' He has no answer and feels hurt, deserted.

Every day Nora and Christine take the Jeep down to the harbour and then one of the beaches. 'Kaspar, want to come along?' Kaspar stays behind, as does Cat, not even asked, immobile in the blue chair. 'All right then, see you later.' Not the slightest note of disappointment in Nora's voice; she guides the Jeep in a serpentine line down the meadow to the little sandy road, Christine waving exaggeratedly. For two or three minutes you can hear the car's engine, then there's silence.

Kaspar lies down in the hammock and looks at Cat through the mesh. Cat draws in his left leg, extends the right one, scratches his head, sits still again. He'll stay till evening, till Nora and Christine come back. He'll stay till after supper, and presumably he'll sleep here too, that's what he did yesterday, on the old sofa in the kitchen. Cat's sleeping in Kaspar's house is something new. It doesn't bother Kaspar. The islanders come, stay uninvited for a day or two, disappear again. It's the custom. Kaspar could go to Brenton's house, lie down in his bed, stay there four days, and then go home again; Brenton wouldn't ask any questions. And Kaspar doesn't ask Cat any questions either. But he wants to know whether Cat is thinking about Christine, or about Nora. Christine?

Christine and Nora watch Cat while he eats. Cat eats everything with the same expression on his face, a stoic fork-to-mouth motion with his head slightly bent toward the plate, his left hand lying flat on the table while he holds the fork in his right.

He eats everything without betraying the least emotion, and never says this is good or that tastes funny. 'He eats because he's hungry,' Christine thinks, 'because you eat to satisfy hunger, and that's all.' She watches him, and sometimes he looks at her with half-closed eyes until she lowers her gaze. She puts rice on his plate, akee and salt fish. She likes putting food on Cat's plate.

The evenings are long, and Christine becomes restless. Nora lies in the hammock, plays the didgeridoo, blowing long, hollow, vibrating tones out into the night. She does this for hours, and won't allow herself to be distracted even by Christine, who walks back and forth on the porch, arms crossed over her chest, nervous and bored. 'Kaspar, why do you live here?'

Kaspar is on the lawn, watering the azaleas. Christine, an intent expression on her face, leans against one of the porch columns six feet away from him. Kaspar doesn't like these questions. He doesn't like Christine's restlessness, but still he says, 'I guess because I'm happy here. Happier than elsewhere, I mean.'

'How come?' says Christine, trying to listen to him, though she's already bored again.

'Look around you,' Kaspar says, straightening up and pointing toward the jungle, toward the ocean, the fiery glow in the mountains, down in the inlet the misty, orange-coloured lights of the harbour. Christine follows his glance. Kaspar remembers how, on the first night after her arrival, she sat on the porch, her knees drawn to her chest, and stared into the darkness for a really long time, very quiet.

'All right,' she now says defiantly. 'All right, I know. But still, you must miss something. Autumn, for all I know, snow and the changing seasons; you're not a native. I mean, you must miss the city, your friends, your old apartment, all that – don't you miss all that?'

'No, I don't,' Kaspar says, sounding annoyed.

Christine slowly slides off the porch and walks along behind him.

'What do they talk about here anyway, Kaspar. I wouldn't want to spend my life talking about papayas and breadfruit. About mangoes. Sex, children.'

'You don't have to,' Kaspar says. Christine replies, 'One has to make up one's mind,' then turns and runs down across the meadow.

'Christine!' Kaspar calls after her in an attempt to be conciliatory. 'The hang glider pilot is coming tomorrow!' Christine, already out of sight, calls back, 'And when is the goddamn hurricane coming?'

The hang glider pilot arrives early in the morning, but the islanders are already there. They must have started out at dawn, because when the hang glider pilot's small red car comes crawling up the mountain the villagers from Stony Hill and Snow Hill are already gathered on the porch, silent. 'Flyman,' Cat says, as always sitting in the blue chair, and starts to laugh, Christine watches him out of the corner of her eye. Nora squats in the shade, smokes Craven 'A's and drinks black coffee; the hang glider pilot unfolds plastic tarpaulins, pulls out rods, perspires, inserts metal into metal.

It is hot. The sun beats down, and there is almost no wind. Kaspar wonders how the flyman is planning to lift off here, down the hill all the way to the harbour: he has picked the big taxi parking lot as his landing site. The flyman puts on a helmet and climbs into a harness bundle resembling a sleeping bag. 'Flying bag,' Kaspar thinks. The flyman now looks like an angry giant insect just before it emerges from its strange cocoon, and on the porch suppressed merriment is spreading.

'Flyman fly,' Nora sings softly. Christine squats down next to her and giggles. Eagles are ascending over the hill, and far out at sea a ship is blinking. Cat gently shoos away the flies and closes his eyes. The flyman starts to run, the grass rustling under his flying harness bundle. The glider lifts off, a murmur passes through the ranks of the spectators from Stony and Snow Hill, the eagles above the hill soar and glide. The flyman rears up, the harness bundle flaps, the glider flies for twelve feet and then, with a dull thump, drops down into the reeds at the edge of the meadow.

Someone gets up and runs into the house. Christine says, 'I'm going to take a shower'; morning turns into noon, unnoticed. The ship far out at sea changes course and heads for the harbour. Nora is standing in the kitchen, squeezing mangoes and guavas and breaking ice into small pieces. Christine is singing in the shower; Cat in the blue chair lowers his head and opens his eyes. The islanders go around to the back of the house with Kaspar to check out the new goats, a light breeze blows from the mountains. The flyman kneels again, the glider rattles and rises. It rises three feet, then six, it shimmers blue, rises further, glides in a straight beautiful line over the meadow towards the jungle, glides at an angle, rises higher and higher. Only Cat sees it disappear, a small pair of wings above the trees, a steel strut catches the sunlight, glitters briefly, then it is gone, merging with the blue of the sea; Cat sees the ship, now nearly at the entrance to the harbour, a white banana freighter that will be heading for England.

'You must learn to wait,' Cat says that evening; Nora and Christine are disappointed because they didn't see the flyman's take-off. 'For minor events too.' Christine stares at him: it is the first time that Cat has ever spoken to her, and she doesn't know whether she should consider it impertinent. She says, 'What do you mean – minor events?' Cat doesn't answer, but Kaspar laughs and says, 'Slow motion. Like a ship on the ocean.' Christine leaves the kitchen, insulted.

The radio station has increased the number of its hurricane reports to twelve a day. In Costa Rica the first evacuation measures are being taken; the Germans down in the port are contacting their embassy and booking flights to the United States. The eye of the hurricane, Kaspar says, is stationary. He buys alcohol, candles, gas, iodine and adhesive tape, canned meat and rice.

'When the hurricane comes,' Christine says hesitantly, 'I won't be able to fly home.' Nora, who wants to stay longer anyway, says nothing.

Cat waits seventeen days. On the eighteenth day he leaps out of the blue porch chair and grabs Christine, who, with paper and pen in one hand and a cigarette between her lips, is about to go inside; he holds her by the wrist.

He says, 'I like you.' His voice sounds rough and unused. Christine stops in her tracks, takes the cigarette from her mouth with her free hand, and stares at him: his eyelashes curve upward in an unreal sweep, the whites of his eyes are yellow from smoking hashish, his face is very close to hers. Christine shudders; he smells good.

Cat repeats, 'I like you,' and Christine laughs quite suddenly and says, 'Yes, I know,' twists her wrist out of his grasp and runs into the house.

Kaspar says, 'Cat has a wife and child.'

Christine, barefoot, her knees, as so often, drawn up close to her body, is sitting next to him on the porch, scraping the remaining pulp from a mango pit. She says, 'I know. Brenton told me.'

23

Kaspar says, 'And what are you doing about it now that you know?'

Christine lowers the mango pit and looks at him with irritation. 'Nothing. What should I do about it – I simply know. I suppose I don't care.'

Kaspar says, 'His wife's name is Lovey. She isn't here. Two weeks ago she went back to her family because Cat started something with another woman.'

Christine picks at the mango pit, licks her fingers and looks absentmindedly down toward the harbour. 'Brenton says Cat would deny it.'

Kaspar kicks the pit out of her hand and expects her to be indignant, but Christine doesn't react. The pit falls into the grass. Kaspar says, 'That's not the point,' but he might as well be shouting into Christine's ear; he has the feeling she isn't really listening to him. 'Lovey was going to come back after a week, but she isn't back yet, not even today. Cat is waiting. Whether he lies about it or not, he's waiting, you see. For her and for his child.'

'Waiting for minor events, right,' Christine says cynically, then suddenly looks straight at Kaspar with childlike surprise. 'He would never go after her to get her back, right?'

'No,' Kaspar says. 'That isn't – usually done. He would never go to fetch her, but still he's waiting. When she comes he'll go home.'

Christine fishes the pit out of the grass and feels a brief pain in her stomach. 'He says he likes me.'

'I know,' Kaspar says, getting up. 'You are what they call "a white lady" here. It's isn't about you, it's about your skin colour. You should keep out of this.' Christine shrugs and puts her head on her knees.

The banana freighter stays in the harbour for a week. Kaspar wonders whether the long layover has something to do with the hurricane reports; the bananas were loaded a long time ago, but the sailors are still hanging out on the docks, scrubbing the deck, lying around in the shade, sitting motionless and silent in the bars. They look Mongolian, almost like Eskimos, their faces round and dark, their eyes slanted. Nora and Christine sit on the pier and look up at the huge white ship. In spite of the heat the sailors up there on deck are wearing red coveralls with hoods they've pulled over their heads.

'They're going to Costa Rica and Cuba,' Christine says. 'Past America to Europe. I would love to travel on a ship like that sometime. Now. We could ask them if they'd take us along.'

Nora says nothing. She looks up at the Mongolian sailors, would like to be able to see their eyes properly. Christine leans her head on Nora's shoulder and feels close to tears.

'Oh, Christine,' Nora says. 'We're here on holiday. Visiting, understand? That's all. You pack your suitcase, and three, four weeks later you unpack it again. You arrive and stay and leave again, and what is making you sad is something entirely different. You'll be flying home soon, and we're not going to sail to Cuba and Costa Rica on that banana freighter.'

'Are you coming back with me?' Christine asks, and Nora says, 'No. I think I'll stay with Kaspar a little longer.' Christine looks at her sideways, then says, 'Why?' and narrows her eyes.

Nora shrugs. 'Maybe I feel sorry for him? Maybe I owe him something because of what used to be? Maybe I think he needs some company? I don't know. I'm simply staying.'

Christine repeats, 'You're simply staying,' then laughs, says, 'Belafonte's "Jamaica Farewell", do you know it? "Sad to say, I'm on my way, won't be back for many a da-ay."'

'"My heart is down, my head is turning around,"' Nora sings and giggles. 'Cat. What's with Cat?'

'I don't know,' Christine says. 'I come and stay and leave again. What should there be.'

That evening when Cat sits down on the porch next to Christine, Kaspar and Nora get up. Christine turns toward them, surprised, wants to say something, says nothing. They go into the house and pull the door shut behind them. Cat sits next to her and is silent. Christine is silent too. They look down across the meadow; in the jungle fires are lit, there is scarcely a breeze. Christine feels Cat's hand on her head, he's tugging at the elastic holding her hair; it tweaks a bit, her braid is loosened, and her hair falls over her shoulders. Cat twists a strand around his finger and smooths it, Christine gets goosepimples on her arms and neck. Cat puts his hand on the back of her neck. Christine bends her head forward and closes her eyes, the very gentle pressure of Cat's hand at the nape of her neck, and she feels dizzy. 'One night,' Cat says. 'No,' Christine says. 'That's not possible.' She gets up and takes back her hair elastic. Cat laughs quietly and softly slaps his thigh with the flat of his hand. Nora and Kaspar are sitting in the kitchen not talking; they look tense. 'Thanks,' Christine says to them. 'Thanks a lot, that really wasn't necessary. Shit.' She slams the door to her room behind her and bolts it shut.

'Lucky,' Kaspar says, and Nora asks, 'Who was lucky. Christine or Cat?'

Two days later Lovey comes back. She suddenly turns up at the edge of the hill and stops there; she is accompanied by two women, one holding a white parasol over her, the other carrying a child in her arms. Lovey stands there, immobile, and looks up toward the house. Cat is sitting on the blue porch chair, his eyes as usual half closed; it isn't clear whether he even sees her. Nora and Christine, on their way to the beach, stop beside the Jeep and stare at Lovey. 'That's her,' Christine thinks, feeling strangely breathless. The second woman impassively holds the parasol over Lovey's head. Lovey stares up at the house, arms crossed over her chest, and makes no attempt to come closer. Cat seems to hold out against this. Nora and Christine stand still and don't move. Then Cat gets up and jumps down off the porch, his face grim; he walks stiffly toward Lovey, five steps, seven, twelve, Christine is counting. Directly in front of Lovey he stops.

The white parasol sways a bit. Lovey says something, Cat replies. They stand facing each other. 'What did she say, what did she say?' Christine whispers, and Nora hisses, 'I couldn't hear!'

Cat turns and goes back to the house. Lovey turns her head and looks at Nora and Christine. 'She's putting a spell on us!' Nora whispers, pinching Christine's arm, Christine feels her heart leap. Lovey grabs the parasol and closes it; the three women swing their hips and disappear as suddenly as they came.

Cat sits down in the blue chair. Christine goes out on the porch every five minutes, circles around him, waters the azaleas, clears her throat, moves chairs around, carries coconuts into the house. Cat doesn't react. He sits there like that for two hours, then he gets up and without saying a word walks to the back of the house. Christine knows he's taking the shortcut to Stony Hill, the one you can only take with a machete in your hand and rage in your belly.

The game is called 'Imagining a Life Like That'. You can play it in the evening when you're sitting at Brenton's Place on the step that leads up to his store, in the dark, with cigarettes and a glass of rum and Coke. You can play it if you have a little sleeping child in your arms, a child whose frizzy hair smells of salt. Nora imagines Brenton standing behind the worn counter. Christine chooses Cat, who, since Lovey came back, no longer sits on Kaspar's porch, but instead plays dominoes with the old men or retreats to the bamboo bench far back at the edge of the clearing.

'Imagine,' Nora says. 'Imagine the child in your arms is your own. It is tired after a long hot day. Cat is your husband. He's playing a game of dominoes and drinking a little rum. You rock your child and wait till Cat is finished, then you walk home on the Stony Hill road. There are no street lamps, only the stars above you. Cat carries the child and walks in front; he is of course very strong because he works in the fields all day. You walk like that through the night into the jungle, and from time to time he has to clear the path with his machete, you're impressed by that.' Nora takes a deep breath. Christine shuffles her feet and says impatiently, 'Go on!'

'Well,' Nora says. 'Of course the two of you don't talk, what is there to say to Cat? He's the best goat butcher, the strongest worker, he has a hut in the mountains and some money under his mattress. That's a lot. You're quite happy with him, not least because the women in the village envy you for him. When you reach your hut, you put the child to bed and then you make love. In the dark, probably. Then you fall asleep, tomorrow is another day, and that you once ... you've forgotten that.'

Christine smokes, listens, and looks at Cat. He's playing dominoes, and now and then he looks up and gives her the hint of an aggressive smile. Nora rubs spit on the mosquito bites on her legs and scratches them with relish. She says, 'Go on. It's your turn.'

'And when all of us have gone,' Christine says, 'you kiss Brenton, turn off the radio, close the shutters, and it becomes quiet. You put away the glasses and the rum and count the day's takings. You wonder whether the next thing you want to buy is a refrigerator or, after all this time, a very small television set. Brenton is a good man. He sells rum, cigarettes, bread, adhesive tape, paper and pencils. People say he has a lot of money under his mattress; you would know if that's true. Brenton is gentle, and has never had a fight with anyone; people also say you have him under your thumb. No matter – he loves you very much, and most of all he loves your hair and the little white hollow at the base of your throat. You chase the chickens out of the hut, bring in the dogs, smoke another cigarette, and then turn out the light. I think you sleep on small cots at the back of the store; I know the child sleeps in the compartment on the right side under the counter. Brenton snuggles up against your back and puts his arms around you, you fall asleep, and everything – is all right.'

Nora laughs, and Christine nudges her with her shoulder. The child in her arms is breathing quietly and moves its hands in sleep.

The hurricane brushes Costa Rica, destroys some hotel facilities and causes a tidal wave in which two fishermen lose their lives. Then it moves back out to sea again and becomes stationary one hundred and twenty-five miles north of the Island. Christine sits at the foot of the hill and watches the horizon. The radio is still issuing hurricane reports twelve times a day. The tourists in the clubs, so the islanders say, left days ago. The embassy phones to ask if Kaspar wants to book a flight to the United States, but he says no. He is restless; spends less time than usual working in the fields; instead repairs the roof and the shutters, carries water and coconuts down into the cellar. The people from Stony Hill and Snow Hill come with baskets on their heads and store them in the house.

'I want it to come,' Christine says sitting at the foot of the hill, her hand shielding her eyes, the sky white and cloudless. 'I want the hurricane to come, damn it all.'

'If it does come, you'll shit in your pants, damn it all,' says Kaspar, who is standing behind her. He looks at the back of her neck; she has become tanned, the skin on her shoulders is peeling. 'You'll be wailing and blubbering. A hurricane isn't a melodrama. A hurricane is terrible. You may want it to relieve you of having to make decisions, but not at the expense of the Island, not at my expense.'

Christine turns around and looks exaggeratedly surprised. Kaspar's face is white and he is biting his lips.

'Look here,' Christine says softly, furiously, 'what's this all about?'

'I called the airline,' Kaspar whispers in reply. 'It's no problem at all for you to leave in two days, they'll be flying out till the end of this week. Only then, only after you're back home, will it start.'

Christine does not answer. The grass under her naked feet is prickly and stiff. I'd like to have soles like Cat's, she thinks, soles like a hard rind, and no step I take would hurt anymore. Nora is standing on the porch, is watching her, Christine sits there and doesn't move, and Nora turns around and walks into the house.

Of course Christine kissed Cat that last evening. Kaspar didn't want to drive to Brenton's, but Christine and Nora did, so they went. Kaspar drove the Jeep down the rocky road, the white beams of the headlights eerie in the total darkness; a huge moth smashed into the windshield, and Christine reached for Nora's hand. Down at Brenton's the children were just coming back from a soccer game, the old men were playing dominoes, Brenton had a new refrigerator, and Cat was nowhere to be seen.

Christine, feeling restless and sad, stared nervously at all the black faces. She wanted to drink some dark rum, quickly. 'Bee-uutiful refrigerator, Brenton,' and Brenton laughed, was very proud, put all the Coke bottles into the freezer compartment where after six minutes they froze into fat brown lumps. 'Is Cat here?' Christine asked, looked pleadingly at Kaspar. He didn't answer. Nora presumed Cat was sitting on the bamboo bench; someone seemed to be sitting there, a shadow, not quite recognizable.

Christine drank some rum, smoked one cigarette after another, and was unable to really listen to anybody. Out of the darkness, off and on, came the metallic snapping of a cigarette lighter. Christine understood only after the fourth time, then ran off toward the bamboo bench – 'Cat?' Cat showed his white teeth, and Christine sat down beside him, breathless, her heart pounding. She leaned against him, said nothing.

Nora and Kaspar, outside in the clearing, in the bright glow of the lamp on the step in front of the store. Brenton was busying himself with his refrigerator while the children squatted around Nora and pulled on her long smooth hair.

'Will you come again?' Cat asked. Christine instantly said, 'Yes,' lied effortlessly, tried, leaning against him, to figure out what he smelled like – petroleum, earth, rum, hashish? All strange. The old men slapped their dominoes down on the table, and a child secured herself a place on Nora's lap. The world was divided in two. Christine dangled her legs, then Cat took hold of her head and kissed her. She realized with amazement that his jaw cracked as he did, and the 'Imagining a Life Like That' game passed through her thoughts like a bright red strip of paper.

She kissed Cat and thought her mouth was much too small for his; Cat's jaw cracked and, as he was kissing her, he looked over towards the store with wide open eyes. When Brenton looked up he let go of her. Kaspar turned around and spoke with Brenton. Nora stealthily craned her neck, and Christine knew that she was trying to see what was going on on the bamboo bench.

'When you come back, will that be our time?' Cat asked. Christine answered, 'Of course, that will be our time,' lying again. She thought of the Island, as if for the first time. Would she live in Cat's house, or where? And Lovey? And Cat's child? For four weeks or five? She kissed Cat and carefully touched the inside of his hand with a finger. The rum that was left in the glass tasted sweet and burned her throat. Confused, Christine thought that drinking rum on the Island was completely different from drinking rum back home, and she heard Kaspar calling her name. Cat held on to her, didn't close his eyes this time either, then Christine freed herself, and called back, 'Yes?' in a voice that sounded strange even to her. Cat didn't say goodbye either; she jumped off the bench and took a seat in the jeep. Kaspar stared at her reproachfully, and she turned away.

The taxi that will take her to the airport arrives at four o'clock in the morning, and up until three Christine keeps thinking that Nora will come into the room, stand there sleepy-faced – 'Christine, I'll come with you after all.'

But Nora doesn't come. Christine sits on the sofa, falls asleep, wakes up again, and the wind blows around the house; now opening the door again and sitting on the porch one more time – in Cat's blue chair? – is not possible anymore. Christine writes a note to Nora and stuffs it into the didgeridoo. At four o'clock the beams of the taxi's headlights finger their way up the hill;

the sun will be rising above the ocean soon. Christine puts her backpack into the trunk, sits down next to the driver and buckles her seatbelt. The driver, too tired to talk, asks only, 'Airport?' Christine nods and closes her eyes.

Later Nora writes to Christine: *The hurricane passed us by, now the sun shines all day long, and we've eaten up Kaspar's emergency rice. Cat misses you and says you'll be coming back soon; I say – yes.*

Sonja

Sonja was pliable. I don't mean pliable like a willow twig; it was not a physical thing. Sonya was pliable – mentally. It's hard to explain. Maybe it was because – she fitted into all the projections I imposed on her: she fitted in with all my wishful thinking about her, she could be a stranger, a little muse, the woman you meet once on the street and then remember years later with a sense of tremendous loss. She could be stupid and conventional, cynical and clever. She could be splendid and beautiful, and there were moments when she was a little girl, pale in a brown coat and truly insignificant; I think she was so pliable because she was in fact nothing.

I met Sonja on the train from Hamburg to Berlin. I had been visiting Verena and was on my way home; I had spent eight days with Verena, and I was very much in love with her. Verena had cherry-red lips and raven-black hair that I would plait into two thick braids every morning. We went for walks along the harbour, I hopped and skipped around her, shouted her name, shooed away the seagulls, thought she was wonderful. She took pictures of the dockyards, barges and hotdog stands, talked a lot, was constantly laughing at me, and I would sing, 'Verena, Verena,' kiss her cherry-red lips, and want very much to go home and back to work, the smell of her hair on my hands.

It was May. The train was passing through Mark Brandenburg, and the meadows were very green in the long, early-evening shadows. I left my compartment to smoke a cigarette, and there, in the corridor, stood Sonja. She was smoking, her right leg pressed up against the ashtray; as I walked up to her she pulled her shoulders forward involuntarily, and something wasn't quite right about her. The circumstance wasn't unusual – a narrow corridor on an intercity express train somewhere between Hamburg and Berlin, two people accidentally standing next to each other because both wanted to smoke a cigarette. But Sonja was staring doggedly out the window, tense, as though there'd been a bomb alert. She was not at all beautiful. In fact that very first moment she was anything but beautiful, the way she stood there in jeans and a skimpy white shirt; she had shoulder-length, straight, blonde hair, and her face was as unusual and as old-fashioned as one of those Madonna paintings from the fifteenth century – a narrow, almost pointed face. I looked at her out of the corner of my eyes, feeling uncomfortable and annoyed because my memory of Verena's sensuousness was fading. I lit a cigarette and walked down the passageway, smoking; I wanted to whisper an obscene remark in her ear. When I turned to go back to my compartment, she looked at me.

Something ironic came to mind, something like, Well, she dared to look at me after all. The train clattered, and a child screamed in one of the compartments at the back of the car. Her eyes were nothing special, maybe green, not very large, and set pretty close together. I stopped thinking about anything and just looked at her. She looked back at me, a look without a hint of eroticism or flirtation, without sweetness, but with such serious directness that I could have slapped her face. I took two steps towards her, and she smiled just barely. Then I was back in my compartment, pulling the door shut behind me, almost out of breath.

*   *   *

The train stopped at the Zoo station after it was already dark. I got off, felt strangely relieved, and imagined that I could smell the city. It was warm, the platform full of people, and I took the escalator down to the U-Bahn. Although I hadn't been looking for her, I caught sight of her right away. She was three, four yards ahead of me, carrying a small red hatbox in her right hand, her back just one big challenge. I clenched my teeth and ignored her. I stopped at the Press Café to buy tobacco and an evening paper, and then she was standing beside me. She said, 'Shall I wait.'

She didn't ask, she simply said it, looking at the ground, her voice not sounding the least bit embarrassed but firm, and a bit husky. She was very young, maybe nineteen or twenty. My uneasiness dissolved and gave way to a sense of superiority. I said, 'Yes,' without really knowing why, paid for the tobacco and the newspaper, and then we walked side by side to the U-Bahn. The train came, we got on; she was silent, put down her silly hatbox. Just before things became uncomfortable she asked, 'Where are you coming from?' This time it was a real question.

I could have told her that I had been visiting my girlfriend in Hamburg, but for some reason I said, 'I went fishing with my father.'

She stared at my mouth. I wasn't sure whether she'd even been listening to me, but suddenly I knew that she had decided she wanted me. She must have seen me earlier, perhaps in Hamburg, perhaps in Berlin. She knew me even before I had become aware of her, and when I had stood next to her to smoke a cigarette she hunched her shoulders forward because she had decided on her next move. She had planned this, and knew that it would turn out like this, and now she gave me the creeps. I shouldered my backpack and said, 'I have to get off here.' With incredible speed she took a pencil out of her hatbox, wrote something on a piece of paper, and pressed it into my hand – 'You can call me.'

I didn't reply, and got off without saying goodbye. I stuffed the paper into my jacket pocket instead of throwing it away.

May was warm and sunny. I rose early, got a lot of work done in my studio, wrote innumerable letters to Verena. She seldom wrote back, but occasionally she phoned to tell me some story or other, and each time I took pleasure in her voice and her easy-going nature. The linden trees were in bloom in the rear courtyard of my house, and I played soccer with the Turkish boys and longed for Verena, without torturing myself. When it got dark I would take off; it was as if the whole city were slightly intoxicated. I went out drinking and dancing, and there were women I liked, but then I thought of Verena and went home by myself.

Two weeks later I found Sonja's piece of paper in my jacket. She had written her telephone number in large round numerals, and under it just her first name. I said it softly to myself – 'Sonja.' Then I called her. She answered the phone as though she had been sitting next to it for the last two weeks doing nothing but waiting for my call. I didn't have to identify myself; she knew immediately who I was, and we made a date to meet that evening at a café down by the water.

I hung up, with no regrets, then called Verena and shouted cheerfully into the phone that I loved her madly. She giggled and said that she was coming to Berlin in three weeks, then I began to work, whistling the refrain from 'Wild Thing'. Towards evening I left, hands in my pockets, and not the slightest bit nervous.

Sonja arrived half an hour late. I was sitting at the bar and had ordered my second glass of wine when she entered the café. She was wearing an unbelievably old-fashioned red velvet dress, and I noticed with irritation that she was causing a stir. She came traipsing toward me in heels that were much too high, said, 'Hello,' and 'I'm sorry,' and for an instant I was tempted to tell her that I thought she was ridiculous, her get-up, her lack of punctuality, everything about her. But then she grinned, climbed up on a stool, dug her cigarettes out of a tiny backpack, and my anger turned into amusement. I drank my wine, rolled myself a cigarette, grinned back at her, and began to talk.

I talked about my work, my parents, my love of fishing, about my friend Mick, and about America. I talked about people who rustle candy wrappers in the movies, about Francis Bacon and Jackson Pollock and Anselm Kiefer. I told her about Denmark, about the Turkish boys in the rear courtyard, and about the lover my mother had ten years ago, about cooking lamb and rabbit, about soccer, and about Greece. I described Chios and Athens, the breakers in Husum, and the spawning of salmon in the summer in Norway. I could have talked Sonja to death, and she wouldn't have stopped me. She simply sat there, looking at me, her head cradled in her hands, smoking a huge number of cigarettes and drinking a single glass of wine. She listened to me for four hours. Actually I believe she never spoke a single word during all that time. When I was finished, I paid for both of us, said goodnight to her, took a taxi home, and slept deeply and without dreaming for eight hours.

I forgot Sonja immediately. I prepared my show, June came, and Verena arrived in Berlin. She returned my empty bottles for their deposits, bought large quantities of groceries, filled the kitchen with bunches of lilac, and was always ready to go to bed with me. She sang in the apartment while I worked, cleaned my windows, spent hours on the phone with her friends in Hamburg, and kept running into my studio to tell me things. I combed her hair, photographed her from all angles, and began to talk about children and getting married. She was pretty tall, and on the street men would turn to look at her. She smelled wonderful, and I was serious about her.

At the end of the month my show opened. While Verena went to the train station to pick up her friends, I paced restlessly back and forth in the gallery, and rehung one last picture. I was nervous. Towards seven o'clock Verena came back and hustled her friends past my pictures; I left the gallery to be by myself for five minutes. I crossed to the other side of the street, and there, in a doorway, stood Sonja. To this day I don't know whether she had come by chance or whether she had somehow found out about the show. She knew only my first name, and I hadn't told her anything about the gallery. She stood there looking absolutely furious, arrogantly furious in fact, and then she said, 'You were going to call me. You didn't call. I'd like to know why, because I don't think that's right.'

I was really taken aback at this impertinence. I became annoyed and unsure of myself and said, 'My girlfriend is here. I can't split myself in two. I don't want to.'

We stood face to face, staring at each other. I thought she was tactless. The corners of her mouth began to tremble, and I had the feeling that something was going completely wrong. She said, 'Can I come in anyway?' I said, 'Yes,' turned around and went back to the gallery.

Twenty minutes later she came in. By then the place had filled up; she didn't attract any attention, but I still saw her immediately. She came in with a tense expression and a strained haughty look. She seemed very small and vulnerable. She was looking for me; I looked at her and then at Verena, who was standing at the bar. Sonja followed my glance and understood immediately. I wasn't afraid of a scene, as there would have been no grounds for a row. Still, I knew anything was possible but I also knew that nothing would happen. I kept an eye on Sonja as she walked back and forth in front of my pictures; the only thing that gave her away was the fact that she spent half an hour in front of each picture. I sat on a chair watching her, and drank a lot of wine. Now and then Verena came over and said something about being 'proud' of me. I felt pretty good, but beneath it all I sensed a strange uneasiness that I had not known before. Sonja did not look at me again. After she had stood in front of the last picture for a quarter of an hour she marched resolutely toward the door and left.

In July Verena went back to Hamburg. I never tired of her – I was sure I would be able to spend my whole life with her – but when she was gone the bunches of lilac wilted in the kitchen, the empty bottles started piling up again, dust whirled through the studio, and I no longer missed her. For weeks the city was submerged in a yellow light. It was very hot, and I spent hours at a time lying naked on the wooden floor of my room staring at the ceiling. I wasn't uneasy, or on edge, but I was tired and in a strangely emotionless state. Perhaps that was why I phoned Sonja again, even though I thought the whole thing was in fact quite hopeless, but good God, it was the middle of summer. The Turkish women were sitting in the rear courtyard plucking geese, white feathers fluttering up to my window. I dialled Sonja's number and let it ring ten or twenty times. She wasn't home. In any case she didn't answer the phone. I tried again and again, feeling an almost obsessive desire to torment her, to make her suffer. But Sonja evaded me.

*   *   *

She evaded me for almost four months. Not until November did I receive a card from her, forwarded to me by the gallery. It was a black and white photograph of some Chekhovian group, and on the back was an invitation to a party.

I polished my shoes, took a long time deciding whether to wear my leather jacket or my coat, chose the leather jacket, and towards midnight I set out; I was nervous because I was sure I wouldn't know anyone at the party. For a long while I wandered through the factory quarter where Sonja lived at that time. Her house was located between a car crusher and a factory, right on the Spree: it was an old grey apartment house, and except for the brightly lit windows on the fourth floor, it was dark. I staggered up the stairs: the hall light wasn't working. I didn't know whether to laugh or be annoyed; suddenly I felt that it was all an unreasonable imposition. But then I reached the fourth floor. The door to the apartment stood open, someone pulled me into the entrance hall, and there was Sonja, leaning against the wall and looking slightly tipsy. She smiled at me with an absolutely triumphant expression, and for the first time I thought her beautiful. Next to her stood a small woman in a long seaweed-green dress with an incredible abundance of red hair, and Sonja pointed at me and said, 'That's him.'

She had invited about fifty people, though I was sure that only a few of them were really her friends. But the combination of people, faces and characters made me feel that the old apartment house on the Spree was gradually losing its hold on reality. I don't usually have impressions like that, but sometimes – very rarely – there are parties one never forgets, and Sonja's party was one of those. Candlelight came from three or four almost bare rooms, somewhere Tom Waits was singing. I wasn't the least bit drunk, and yet I felt giddy. I went to the kitchen and found myself a glass of wine, and then I wandered through Sonja's rooms and had innumerable peculiar conversations with innumerable peculiar people. Sonja seemed to be everywhere. Wherever I was, she always happened to be standing on the other side of the room, or perhaps I was always wherever she happened to be. She had invited many of her admirers: in any case she was constantly surrounded by changing groups of young men, and usually the red-haired woman was at her side. Sonja drank vodka by the glassful and always had a cigarette in her hand; each of us would be talking with someone or other, and all the while we were looking across at each other over their heads. I think we hardly spoke a single word to each other. It wasn't necessary; she seemed to think it was nice that I was there, and I enjoyed moving around in her apartment and having her watch me.

At some point I saw her standing near the front door of the apartment with a very tall and remarkably ungainly man, leaning against him. I felt a soft twinge in my stomach, and about half an hour later she was gone. She had simply vanished.

The light was turning grey outside the windows. I walked through the apartment, trying to find her, but she was no longer there. The short red-haired woman came up to me, her smile just as triumphant as Sonja's had been hours ago. She said, 'She's gone. She always leaves at the end.' So I finished my wine, put on my jacket and left too. I think I was hoping she would be waiting for me downstairs, a little cold, her hands in the pockets of her winter coat, but of course she wasn't waiting. The Spree looked steely in the morning light, and I stumbled along the street. It was very cold, and I remember that I was very angry.

After that I saw Sonja almost every night. I got up early again, drank two pots of tea, took ice-cold showers, started working.

Towards noon I slept for an hour, then I drank some coffee, read the newspaper, went on working. I was caught up in a high – both wild and cold simultaneously – of pictures and colours; I felt I had never been so clear-headed before. Sonja came very late in the evening; sometimes she was so tired she fell asleep at the kitchen table, but she always came, and she always looked plucky. I cooked for us, we would drink a bottle of wine together, and I would put the studio in order while she softly padded behind me in her stocking feet.

I didn't know Sonja considered it a gift that I let her into my apartment and into my studio, that she could sit at my kitchen table amidst my notes, that she could watch me developing my photos and making little sketches. In her own way she took me very seriously. She would walk into the studio with an almost religious reverence, stand in front of my pictures with the respect of a museum visitor, then sit down at my kitchen table as though she were being granted an audience. She didn't bother me because I wasn't actually aware of any of this at the time. She didn't get on my nerves because she was much too stubborn and tough. I didn't realize that Sonja was in the process of becoming entangled in my life. During these nights she was for me a small, tired person, obsessed by something, who kept me company in her peculiar way, who sat with me, listened to me, gave me a vain feeling of importance.

Sonja never spoke. Practically never. To this day I don't know anything about her family, her childhood, where she was born, her friends. I have no idea what she lived on, whether she had a paying job or whether someone kept her, whether she had professional ambitions, where she was headed and what she wanted. The one person of whom she sometimes spoke was the small red-haired woman I had seen at her party; otherwise she mentioned no one, certainly not men, even though I was sure there were plenty.

During those nights I was the one who talked. I talked as though to myself, and Sonja listened, and often we were silent, and that too was good. I liked her enthusiasm for certain things, for the first snowfall – about which she could go completely overboard, like a child – for an organ concerto by Bach that she played over and over on my record player, for the Turkish coffee we drank after dinner, for riding on the U-Bahn early in the morning at six, or for watching the scenes being acted out at night behind the brightly lit windows across the courtyard. She stole little things from my kitchen – walnuts, chalk, and hand-rolled cigarettes – and kept them in the pockets of her winter coat as if they were sacred objects. Almost every evening she brought along some books that she put on my table, earnestly beseeching me to read them. I never did, and whenever she asked I refused to talk with her about it. When she fell asleep, sitting there, I would let her sleep for fifteen minutes and then wake her with the detachment of a schoolteacher. I would change my clothes and then we would go out, Sonja clinging to my arm, fascinated by our footprints, the only ones in the freshly fallen snow in the courtyard.

We went from one late-night bar to the next, drank whisky and vodka, and sometimes Sonja left my side, sat elsewhere at the bar, and pretended not to know me until, laughing, I called her back. Men would talk to her all the time, but she always withdrew and came back to stand next to me, a proud expression on her face. It didn't matter to me at all. I felt flattered by this odd attractiveness of hers, and watched her with something close to scientific interest. Sometimes, I think, I might have wanted to see her disappear with one of these admirers, but she would stay near me until it got light outside and we left the bar, squinting in the grey strands of morning light. I would bring her to the bus stop and wait until the bus came. She would get on, looking shaky and sad; I would wave briefly and walk on, my thoughts already back on my pictures.

Today, I think I was probably happy those nights. I know that the past always becomes transfigured, that memory has a soothing effect. Perhaps those nights were merely cold and in a cynical way entertaining. Today, though, they seem to me so important and so lost that it grieves me.

During this time Verena was travelling, driving through Greece, Spain, Morocco. She sent postcards of beaches with palm trees and of Arabs on camels, and sometimes she telephoned me. If Sonja happened to be there she would get up and leave the room; she only came back once I had let her know, by making noises and moving chairs around, that the conversation was over. Verena would shout into the phone – the connection was bad most of the time, the roaring of the sea and wind it seemed – and I could use that to cover my sudden lack of words. I didn't forget Verena. I thought of her, and sent letters and photographs to her Hamburg apartment, and was happy with her phone calls. Sonja had nothing to do with that; had someone asked me whether I was in love with her, I would have replied with surprise and certainty – no. Verena, however, thought she could sense changes: she shouted into the phone that I didn't have anything to say to her anymore, she wanted to know how often I betrayed her with other women. I had to laugh, and she hung up.

In January a card mailed from Agadir informed me that she would be arriving at the end of March – *I'm coming in the spring,* she wrote, *and then I'm going to stay for a long time.* I put the card on the kitchen table and waited for Sonja to find it. I knew that, without being blatantly nosy, she habitually went through the notes and papers on my desk. That evening, standing in the doorway, I watched her. She stood at the table, looked at a photo, drew things with my chalks, rolled herself a cigarette, then noticed the postcard, the front of which showed a fireworks display. She read the card and held it in her hand; she stood still, then turned around as though she had known that I was standing there watching her.

'Yep,' I said. She said nothing. She simply stared at me, and I felt something akin to fear. We went out together, and everything was wrong. I felt guilty and was furious. I had the feeling that I should explain something to her but I didn't know what. That night, for the first time, she slept at my place. All that time I had never kissed her, had never touched her: at night we would walk through the streets, arm in arm, and that was all. While I was in the bathroom she put on one of my shirts, and when I came back into the bedroom she was already sitting on my bed, her teeth chattering. It was incredibly cold. I lay down next to her; we lay back to back, only the cold soles of our feet actually touching. Sonja said, 'Goodnight,' her voice soft and small. I felt solicitous and, in an unreal way, moved. I was not at all aroused – nothing could have been further from my thoughts than to make love to her now – yet I felt hurt when I realized, on hearing her calm and regular breathing, that she was already asleep. I lay awake for a long time. It got warm under the covers, and I gently rubbed my feet against hers. I still remember thinking that it would have seemed incestuous to have made love to her, to touch her breasts. I asked myself how it would feel to kiss Sonja, then I fell asleep.

In the morning she was gone. On the kitchen table lay a small torn-off scrap of paper with a few words. I went back to bed and put on the shirt she had worn during the night.

*   *   *

And so she disappeared again. She didn't show up the next evening, nor the evening after that. I waited three evenings, then I began to call her again. But she didn't pick up the phone, or maybe she really wasn't there. I began to prowl through the city in the daytime. In vain I would sit around in cafés that she had sometimes mentioned, and I would stand for hours in front of the old apartment house near the Spree; she had disappeared. There was never a light behind her windows, but her name was still on the door, and the piece of paper I sometimes placed under the door as a means of checking on her movements was moved again and again. In her own way she had given me the slip. By the time March arrived I was tired of looking for her and began to get ready for Verena.

I cleaned up my apartment and tried to blot out all traces of Sonja's visits. But in fact there were no traces. Three months spent with a tired, bewitched little Sonja had left nothing behind; I searched in vain and grew annoyed with myself. For the first time in ages I phoned my friend Mick. We went to shoot some pool and drink beer, danced with various women, and in the course of a week made our way through all the bars in the city. Now and then I would make an attempt to tell him something about Sonja, then I would break off in mid-sentence – actually, what was there to tell? I really didn't know.

At the end of March the last snow melted off the roofs and the swifts returned. I gave the Turkish boys a new soccer ball and cut my hair short. I was waiting for something, but when Verena suddenly stood in front of the door one evening I stopped waiting. I had made it. At night I fell asleep next to Verena, and in the morning woke up next to her. I plaited her hair into braids and gave her an espresso machine as a present. It seemed as though she wanted to stay longer, and I didn't ask how long. I worked, and she walked around the city; in the evenings we went to the movies and sat in the little cafés by the water. Verena hung her things in my closet and started working at a bar around the corner; when my phone rang she would answer it. Mick said she was just about the most beautiful thing he had ever seen, and I agreed with him. The days took on a steady rhythm of their own. I felt well, perhaps even happy, certainly very calm. The linden trees began to bloom in the courtyard, and the first summer thunderstorms gathered over the city; the weather turned hot. Only rarely did I have the feeling that someone was walking close behind me on the street; I would turn around and there'd be no one there, but the feeling of irritation remained. There were moments when I longed for something – I didn't know exactly what, a special event perhaps, some sort of sensation, a change – but this longing would disappear just as suddenly as it had come.

One morning in June, Verena and I rode our bikes down to the outdoor swimming pool by the Spree. Verena paid for us both, saying she couldn't wait to be by the water, and, looking for an unoccupied spot, walked barefoot ahead of me across the lawn full of sunbathers. Triumphantly she stopped in the tiny bit of shade cast by a birch tree, spread out her towel, and sat down. Sitting right next to her was Sonja.

For an absurd moment my heart beat faster. I thought briefly that this pounding was probably the longed-for change, the skip in the rhythm. I stood still and stared from Verena to Sonja, then Sonja looked up from the book she was reading and saw me and then she saw Verena.

I said, 'Verena, I don't want to sit here,' and glanced at Sonja's face, which looked oddly as though it had been torn open. She had let her hair grow, she was tanned, in a blue bathing suit, and very thin. I felt terribly sorry about all this. Verena's voice came from far away – 'This is the best spot available by the pool.' Apparently she hadn't noticed anything, and I felt a trembling in my head. Sonja stood up very slowly, slipped like a sleepwalker into a red dress, and turned to go. Verena said something; I no longer understood the words. But I heard no note of suspicion in her voice so I dropped my bag on the ground next to her and simply followed Sonja. I caught up with her at the exit of the swimming pool. She was walking quickly and erect and looked like a little red stick from behind. I almost ran, then I was at her side holding her by the arm. Her skin was hot from the sun. She turned her crazily serious face toward me and said, 'Do we want to see each other or don't we.'

The tone of her voice was the same as it had been at the train station when she had said, 'Shall I wait.' I felt like an idiot, completely mixed up, then I said, 'Yes,' and she said, 'Well then,' freed herself and walked through the gate into the street. I watched till she disappeared then I returned to Verena who was lying on her back sunning herself and hadn't caught on to any of it. The grass where Sonja had been sitting was crushed; I stared at the two or three cigarette butts she had left behind and fought against the sensation of having lost control.

I didn't have to send Verena away – I wouldn't have done that in any case, I would have just met Sonja in secret. Verena left of her own accord. She claimed that she didn't want to disturb me in the current phase of my work, whatever that might mean; she packed her things, gave notice at the bar, and went back to Hamburg. I think she had had enough of me for a while. She had wanted to make sure that I loved her, she was reassured, and so she left. I took her to the train, feeling shattered and strangely sentimental. I said, 'Verena, anytime,' and she laughed and said, 'Yes.'

That summer was Sonja's summer. We went rowing on the lakes outside the city, and I rowed Sonja on the mirror-smooth, reed-green water until my arms hurt. In the evenings we ate at little village inns – cold cuts and beer, Sonja with red cheeks and sun-bleached hair. We went back on the train, carrying bunches of field flowers that Sonja took home with her. I worked infrequently, studied maps of the surrounding area and wanted to go swimming in all the lakes. Sonja always dragged along a backpack full of books, reading to me and reciting one poem after the other. The evenings were warm, we counted our mosquito bites, and I taught her how to whistle by blowing on a blade of grass. The summer was a chain of bright, blue days; I immersed myself in it and didn't stop to wonder. We spent the nights at Sonja's apartment. From her big tall windows one could see the Spree. We didn't make love, we didn't kiss, we scarcely touched, in fact we never touched. I said, 'Your bed is a ship,' Sonja did not answer – as usual – but the whole summer long she had a triumphant look about her.

It was the end of July. We were sitting in the tiny, empty station in Ribbeck, waiting for a train back to the city, when Sonja opened her mouth and said, 'Sooner or later you're going to marry me.'

I stared at her and killed a mosquito on my wrist; the sky was reddish, and a blue mist hung over the forest. I said, 'Excuse me?' and Sonja said, 'Yes. Marry me. Then we'll have children and everything will be all right.'

I thought she was incredibly stupid. I thought she was ridiculous and stupid, and nothing seemed more absurd than marrying

Sonja and having children with her. I said, 'Sonja, that's ridiculous. You of all people ought to know better. How are we supposed to do that – have children? We're not even sleeping together.'

Sonja got up, lit a cigarette, kicked some pebbles, and crossed her arms. 'Well, for that we'll do it. But only for that purpose. It will work, I know it.'

I got up too. I felt as though I had to talk some sense into a silly child. 'You've lost your marbles, Sonja. What's with this nonsense – everything will be all right? What's that supposed to mean? Everything *is* all right, and so we won't get married.'

The rails began to vibrate. A high note hung suspended in the air, and in the distance a train came into view. Sonja stamped her left foot, threw away her cigarette, and stubbornly marched toward the tracks. She jumped off the station platform, stumbling in the gravel, and finally positioned herself, legs akimbo, across the rails. The train came closer, and I sat down again. Sonja, wild with rage, screamed, 'Are you going to marry me, yes or no?'

I had to laugh and shouted back, 'Sonja dearest! Yes! I'll marry you whenever you say!' And Sonja laughed too, the train came rushing toward us, the air smelled of metal. I said her name, very softly and scared stiff, then she jumped from the tracks back up on the platform, the train roared past, and she said, 'I don't want to right now, you know. But later. Later on I'll want to.'

In the autumn we saw each other less often, then she went away for a while. One morning she was standing at my front door, already wearing her winter coat. She said, 'Hello dear, I have to go away on a trip, but I'd like to have a cup of tea first.'

I let her in and put water on to boil. She walked through my apartment and seemed restless. I asked her where she was going. She said she had to work for a month, then she would come back;

as usual she obviously didn't want to tell me anything. We drank our tea in silence, then she got to her feet, pulled me up by the hands and threw her arms around me.

I held her tight, I couldn't properly defend myself against her earnestness. She said, 'Take care of yourself.' And then she left.

Everything that happened after that happened out of fear. I think I was afraid of Sonja, afraid of what had suddenly become clear to me, the possibility of spending my life with a strange little person who didn't talk, who didn't sleep with me, who mostly stared at me wide-eyed, about whom I knew hardly anything, whom I probably loved, because, after all, I did.

I felt that I no longer wanted to be without Sonja. I found her unexpectedly indispensable, and I missed her. I was afraid she would never come back, and at the same time I wanted nothing so much as that she would stay away, forever.

After the month had passed, I packed a small suitcase and took a train to Hamburg. I breathlessly proposed marriage to a completely surprised Verena, and she accepted. I stayed three weeks, travelled with her to see my parents, and announced our wedding would be in March of the coming year. Verena booked a honeymoon trip to Santa Fe, introduced me to her appalling mother, and informed me that she wouldn't assume my name. It was all the same to me. I felt as if I were drowning, yet I was infinitely relieved. I felt I had escaped from an immense danger at the very last moment, and imagined myself saved, safe. We argued a little about where we would live. Verena wanted me to move to Hamburg, and I said as far as I was concerned everything could stay as before, married or not, and then I went back to Berlin.

*   *   *

There was no mail in my mailbox, and in the studio there was the usual dust on the pictures and the windows were covered with cobwebs. No news of Sonja. I had the situation under control: I had avoided the worst, and now I wanted to be generous, conciliatory. Pedalling hard, I cycled to her house, bounded up the stairs whistling. She was at home, and opened the door inattentively, obviously expecting someone else, then she smiled and said, 'Doing well, are you?'

We sat down in one of the large, almost bare rooms, Sonja at the desk, I on an easy chair near the window. Outside the Spree was brown and seagulls soared over the car crusher. Sonja didn't ask me where I had been. Nor did she tell me anything about her trip. She sat at her table, erect and looking only the tiniest bit anxious, and smoked almost obsessively, one cigarette after another.

I talked casually about the weather, my plans for the winter, the new art show at the National Gallery; I felt safe. Sonja mentioned the party she planned to give again in November. I said I would like to come, and she smiled stiffly. 'Will you go away with me in the spring?' she suddenly asked. I, who had waited all this time, almost brimming with anticipation of finally being able to come out with it, offered her my prepared sentence, loudly, clearly, well articulated, and above all politely: 'That won't be possible because I'm going to marry Verena in March.'

That's when she threw me out. She stood up, pointed to the door with her outstretched arm and said, 'Out.'

I said, 'Come on, Sonja, what's that supposed to mean?' and she repeated, 'Out,' without changing her expression. I started to laugh, I wasn't sure whether she was serious, and then she screamed, 'Out!' in a voice I had never heard her use before. I got up uncertainly. I no longer knew what I had expected. I didn't want to leave, no, not at all; I wanted to see Sonja lose her composure, I wanted her to cry and go on screaming and maybe hit me and I don't know what else.

But Sonja sat down again, turned her back on me, and stayed like that. I shifted from one foot to the other. It was quiet, and the river was disgustingly brown. I breathed, and nothing happened, and then I left, closing the door behind me. I listened – nothing. No outburst, no suppressed sobbing. Sonja didn't ask me to come back.

I cycled home, very slowly; I was – surprised. I had thought that our relationship would probably go on, would somehow go on.

Sonja didn't call, and that, at least, I had expected. It was a game, I knew the rules. I waited a week, then called her, naturally she didn't answer the phone. I wrote her a letter, then another, then a third; lots of light, foolish chatter and helpless excuses. Of course she didn't answer. I remained calm, I was familiar with this sort of thing. I thought, 'Give her time.'

I called her regularly three times a week, allowed the phone to ring ten times, then hung up. I worked, talked on the telephone with Verena, went out with Mick, dialled Sonja's number the way one brushes one's teeth or looks into the mailbox every morning. I was amused and proud of Sonja, proud of the tenacity with which she eluded me, but I also thought that the time had come to stop this foolishness. I wanted to see her. The weather was turning cold, and the first snow fell. I thought of the previous winter, of the nights she had sat with me, and I wanted to have all that again.

I thought, 'Come on, Sonja, answer the phone. Let's go for a walk. I'll warm up your hands, and everything will be just the way it was.'

*   *   *

But in early December my most recent letter to Sonja was lying in my mailbox. In confusion I looked at my own handwriting and didn't quite know what to make of it until I saw stamped on the back of the envelope 'Addressee moved, no forwarding address'. I stood there in the lobby of my apartment house, uncomprehending. It was cold, and I was freezing. I put the letter back in the mailbox and, lurching from side to side, rode my bicycle through the snow along the river to the factory district; I was pedalling slowly and carefully and refused to think of anything. In front of Sonja's house I chained the bicycle to a lamp-post and looked up at the blind dark windows. No curtains, no light, but that didn't necessarily mean anything. The front door creaked as I pushed it open; a smell of dampness and coal dust hung in the lobby. I had always had the impression that Sonja was the only one who lived here, and I suspected that the house was now completely empty. Nevertheless I climbed the stairs. On the third floor the railing had broken away, and the steps creaked alarmingly. I thought back to the party, the babble of voices, the music, Sonja standing next to the little red-haired woman in the seaweed-green dress. The name card next to her apartment door had been torn off. I pushed the doorbell; silence. I peeped through the keyhole into the long, white-painted, empty hallway of her apartment, and I knew that she was gone.

I'm sure the house will soon be torn down. It is February. I keep putting coal into the stove, but it doesn't get any warmer. I didn't see Sonja again, and I haven't heard anything more from her. The bare branches of the linden trees in the courtyard tap against my window, and it's time to buy the Turkish boys a new soccer ball. I keep hoping that sometime I'll run into the little red-haired woman so that I can ask her where Sonja is now living and how she's doing. Sometimes, on the street, I have the feeling that someone is walking close behind me, then I turn around and there's no one there, but the sense of irritation remains.

The End of Something

Sophie says, 'That last year she just lay in bed all the time. On the left side of the bed; the right side was my grandfather's. My grandfather was gone, and she would never lie on his side. Out of habit she woke up early, about six in the morning, a narrow strip of sky over the rooftops, antennas and chimneys, the pigeons on the gutters. I don't know whether she saw all that. She lay under heavy feather quilts, her head cradled on three pillows, stucco roses on the ceiling and the bright glass shade of a lamp, reddish glass. Or green. I'm not sure anymore.'

Sophie says, 'Excuse me,' and bites her lips. She looks out of the window. The windows of the café are large, and one can see all of Helmholtz Square. It's empty, bumpy cobblestones glistening in the rain. The wind whirls leaves up into the air, and a grey dog prowls around the corner. Sophie smiles out the window. 'My father would come at nine, make tea and a soft-boiled egg, slice some bread and put it all on her bedside table, the tea on the teapot warmer; she liked its candlelight. And then she would scold and nag and accuse him, year after year after year. He would never answer her back, but just leave. He lived only two houses down the street, very close. In the summertime he could wave to my grandmother from his balcony but she never waved back. She'd eat by herself, there above the morning rooftops, antennas and chimneys, then she'd lie down again, and look into the tealight of the little warmer till it went out. She would lie there like that till evening came, sleeping or lying there awake. It could be that

59

there was no longer any difference, the hours flowing one into another, the light wandering through the room, no clock on the table, towards evening the strip of sky over the rooftops grey-blue moving into black.'

Sophie looks up at the sky over Helmholtz Square, as though to compare. The sky over Helmholtz Square is pale and heavy with rain. Sophie turns away and looks around the café, holding the coffee cup with both hands. She still looks cold. She squeezes her eyes shut and clears her throat, her expression rather reserved, distant. She says, 'Then my mother would arrive, warm up my grandmother's dinner, wash her laundry, see to the stove in winter, make the bed. My grandmother would put on her sweater, stockings, slippers; with her walker she would push herself like a turtle into the living room and sink into the sofa, turn on the television set. She was given one pack of cigarettes a day. Three cans of beer and three glasses of schnapps, and she always hid the three cans of beer under her behind, pretended she hadn't been given any, simply wanted more beer. She would say to my mother, her daughter, "You begrudge me everything." My mother would pull the beer cans out from beneath my grandmother without saying a word. She would look around in the kitchen for another hiding place for the schnapps bottle that my grandmother – at night? on all fours? in pain, in the morning light, with clenched teeth and groaning? or triumphant? – always found anyway.'

Now Sophie laughs. A little. She laughs and looks into her coffee cup. 'Just imagine it. She could no longer walk – she could only crawl and drag herself around with her walker – but she found the schnapps no matter where it was hidden. Way at the back of the closet, in the pocket of a coat hanging on the coat rack, in the oven, between the flowerboxes on the balcony: she would find it and drink it all and put the empty bottle outside the apartment door. I think she saw it as a sort of game. She always won. Always.'

It's getting dark outside, beginning to rain. Drizzle, maybe snow already. Somebody walks past the big window, hands in the pockets of his coat, shoulders hunched. He slows down and looks in at Sophie, but she doesn't notice. She says, 'I'd like to have some wine.' She says, 'Okay? We'll have some wine in a bit. In any case, my grandmother would then eat whatever my mother put before her, sighing as she did so and continually pressing her left hand to her breast. She was fat and heavy, and her fingers were twisted with gout. My mother would sit next to her and they would watch television, and then they would smoke a cigarette together, and my grandmother would say, "Twilight hour." When my mother got ready to leave my grandmother would break out in tears and become childish and angry and cling to her, threatening and yelling, and my mother would sit down again, but then finally she would go. Sometime during the night, when it snowed on the television screen and all the lights had gone out in the street, my grandmother would push herself back into the bedroom with the walker. Would sit down on the edge of the bed and stare into the dark and think, I don't know about what, would lie down and then fall asleep. Day after day. In the summer she sometimes had a beer on the balcony among the geraniums, to which she would whisper conspiratorially. We washed her hair once a week; then, crouched over the tub she would giggle and say, "It itches so much, oh that feels good." She wet her bed and then lay there crying and miserable till evening. But sometimes she sang and winked with her left eye and laughed about something we knew nothing about, laughed till the tears came. She never listened to music. She would lie in the stillness among the pillows on her bed, in the stillness that had once been noisy, back when her two children were still there and her husband.'

Sophie looks about her. At this hour, between late afternoon and evening, the café is quite empty. Candles burn on the tables where no one is sitting, and the waitress leans against the bar smoking a cigarette, her eyes half closed. 'Is she listening to us?' Sophie whispers. She pulls her chair closer to the table and cradles her chin in both hands. The waitress doesn't move. Rain beats against the window panes, outside the sound of a car engine that refuses to start. Sophie says resolutely, 'In that final year my grandmother was suspicious of the whole world. She saw men in the corner behind the stove, and she would hide her purse under the mattress, in the bedside table, in a pillow case. "Unpack the things you took from me!" she would scream while my mother was warming up her food in the kitchen, and then she would list all the things my father was supposedly taking out of the apartment every morning – furs and silverware and jewellery and the medals of the grandfathers, money and bankbooks, pots and jars. She would tug at my mother's jacket and say, "Stolen jacket." She would gasp and call for the police, and my mother would just stand there, looking at her without saying a word. And my grandmother would push herself into the kitchen with her walker, check the cabinets and drawers, then break into tears and say, "I don't want to go on." Still, she lay in bed all day and waited.'

'You know,' Sophie said, 'it really isn't easy. To dredge up those memories, bit by bit. I forget so quickly. Especially faces, I always forget faces, in fact I forget them immediately, I can no longer remember the face of my grandmother either. She was always cold. And under her feather quilts she wore wool cardigans, scarves, heavy stockings. In spite of that she'd say, "I want fresh air." Even in winter all the windows in the bedroom had to be open. But in the living room little fan heaters stood all around the sofa, blowing hot air into her face, and she would

say, "I don't know, I'm still cold." Her hair was white. She would
let the egg yolk ooze over her bread in the morning and drink her
tea black, without sugar. There was a telephone in the living room
and another in the bedroom, and sometimes her son would call
from the luminous distance of his villa in the suburbs to inquire
about her health as well as his sister's. My grandmother, lying in
her urine and in pain, would take a deep breath, hold the phone
close to her ear and say into the room, "All right, everything is
all right."'

Sophie gets up, much too quickly, and goes to the toilet. She is
so thin, her legs like little sticks in the heavy wool stockings. She
walks very erect, shoulders held high, stiff-backed. The waitress
watches her and yawns, bored, the coffee machine rumbles. No
one is left in the room; the rain is now a cloudburst, and the candle
on the table is drowning in melted wax. Sophie comes back, sits
down again, lights a cigarette, inhales deeply, watches the smoke.
She looks tired. She says, 'My grandmother used to smoke these
long cigarettes, long, light ladies' cigarettes. She never inhaled,
and she always watched the smoke. Like me. Or, me like her.
She'd knock on the wall with her fist whenever my mother was
too slow for her. Once she sat up in bed, pointed at the back of
her head, where her white hair had become curled, and said, "This
means that I will die soon." Or sometimes, and then always with
her eyes turned to the sky above the rooftops, above the antennas,
"God doesn't want me." She could tell two complete stories, or
maybe we only wanted to hear those two. The war story – the
Russians already on the outskirts of Berlin and my grandmother
on the train fleeing with her children; the train stopping suddenly,
no station, no town or village, and her six-year-old son needing to
pee, "Really had to pee," my grandmother would say as though
uninvolved. So she let him get off, into the open field: the rape was
already in bloom and it was a warm day. My grandmother waited

in the door of the train, and her six-year-old son ran into the yellow rape, yelling childish things, and peed; just then the train started up again, unexpectedly, much too quickly, and the child was left in the rape field, open-mouthed, supposedly wearing a blue sailor suit. I don't know the end of the story. At any rate, he didn't die. The post-war story – the two-room apartment in the summertime, her husband already gone, and geraniums on the balcony, my grandmother, as usual in the kitchen, her daughter and her son in the living room, the daughter and the son shooting pebbles with slingshots. My grandmother was peeling potatoes, slicing cabbage. "Bet I can shoot your eye out," her daughter, my mother, said to the son in the living room. "Bet you can't," said the son, and the daughter, his sister, took aim, shot and hit her target. The daughter screamed. The son didn't scream, and the daughter, my mother, stood in the kitchen doorway, covered her face with her hands and whispered, "I hit his eye, the left one," kept whispering it over and over again. My grandmother got up, potato peel and cabbage slicer falling to the floor, and ran into the living room. There stood her son, the pebble was stuck in the middle of his left eye, stuck there like a stone eye. "So I pulled it out," my grandmother would say, very simply. Her son got glass eyes, five little brown glass eyes to wear in turn, and when the brother and sister quarrelled my mother would toss the glass eyes around the room and say, "Go find them, cripple," and my grandmother would giggle. Why. There were no other stories.'

Sophie looks surprised. Not sad, not yet. She rubs her eyes with both hands, and presses her thumbs to her lids. There's a trace of a smile, just barely. She looks at the waitress who slowly pushes herself away from the bar and sidles over to the table, like a sleepwalker. The waitress, wiping her hands on her apron, says nothing. Sophie says in a totally strange voice, 'I would like a glass of dry red wine,' and the waitress slinks back to the bar;

did she get that? 'We'll see,' Sophie says. 'My grandmother left her
apartment one more time, one last time, when her granddaughter
– not me, the other one – had her eighteenth birthday and her
son rented the Lake Terraces and hired an organ grinder and laid
on a huge buffet. "A little bit of everything," the son said into the
telephone, and my grandmother lay in her bed and looked at the
sky above the rooftops, the antennas, and said, "Yes, I'd like to
come." "You'll need a present," my mother said. "She's going
to be eighteen, you have to give her something. Give me some
money and I'll buy it for you." But my grandmother casually
waved her away with her left hand, saying she already had
a present, not to worry. "Where did you get it?" my mother
asked, "There's no way you can buy anything, you can't even
leave the apartment." My grandmother refused to answer her.
Counted the days. Had her hair washed, the blue dress taken out
of the closet, her good dress she said, "As blue as my eyes". She
stopped nagging. Looked at my father in the morning without
a word, threw money at him from her bed, notes out of the
slits in the mattress, the pillow cases, said, "Take it, I don't
want it anymore." On her granddaughter's birthday she left
her apartment in a wheelchair, carried out and loaded into a
van by three men; while they perspired my grandmother sat in
the wheelchair like a queen, holding a basket in her lap with the
wrapped present inside. "What is it?" She shook her head, almost
indulgently, said, "Oh, just wait and see." We followed the van
in our car, and I could see her, could see her white head pressed
against the window: from time to time she wiped the fogged-up
pane with her hand. The entire journey she looked out of the
window – what did she see? I can't tell. At the Lake Terraces
they wheeled her to the head of the table, between her son and
her granddaughter. Everyone was very cheerful and talked to her
and put plates full of food and glasses of wine in front of her, but

she drank nothing, she ate nothing. She handed the present to her granddaughter, who was sitting next to her with a dutiful, reverent expression on her face. It grew quiet at the table. The son laughed – the grandmother is giving her granddaughter a gift. The granddaughter carefully tore open the wrapping paper, felt the present, then hesitated, pulled the paper off completely and held up a yellow pot lid, already somewhat dented on the edges. "What is it?" she asked – a puzzle, a symbol? She was eighteen years old and she smiled at my grandmother. "It's the cover of the pot you stole from me," said my grandmother, "just like you stole everything else from me." And then, very slowly, she raised her hand and put it over her left eye and turned to her son and looked at him with her right eye. It really was as blue as her good dress.'

The waitress puts the wine on the table and stares at Sophie, Sophie does not stare back. She says, 'Thanks,' and takes a hefty swig of the wine, then wipes her mouth with the back of her hand. The door opens and the wind blows in, the smell of rain, two, three customers in wet coats, their faces flushed. Sophie doesn't turn around. She is no longer cold; she has red cheeks now, and the tiredness around her eyes is gone. 'I'm almost finished. The story is almost over, finished, it won't take much longer, is that okay? Later that night they pushed her in the wheelchair one last time down to the lake. She sat there and stared into the darkness, on the other shore little lights, and the soft lapping of the waves, "What's the point?" said my grandmother, and they brought her back home in the van. She let them put her to bed and turned away from them and said to my mother, who was standing by the door, "Goodnight." The next morning my father came over, made tea and a soft-boiled egg, sliced bread, and put it all in front of her, the tea on the little warmer, the egg yolk already on the bread; "The tealight," said my grandmother, "the tealight," that was all. "But it's already lit," said my father, "look, it's burning." And my grandmother said, "Yes," and closed her eyes. My father left. Went shopping, then back home. He heard the telephone ringing while he was still out on the stairs, ringing incessantly. My father unlocked the apartment door, dropped his shopping bags, took the receiver off the hook and said, "Hello," No answer. He listened some more, wanted to hang up again, but then did hear something after all, from very far away, really far away. Crying? Or screaming? A cry of pain? Actually a rustling, a crackling, something totally unreal, how he suddenly knew – I don't know. He dropped the phone and ran out of the apartment, down the stairs, and out into the street. It was February, just like today, and cold. My father ran fast. Two houses away. He ran. Pushed open the front door, ran up the three flights of stairs, he was probably trembling and also afraid; the apartment door was stuck, I think, he must have dropped the key three or four times. He pushed against the door until it opened. The entry hall was small, and something smelled. The door to the bedroom was ajar and behind it, a bright glow. I no longer know whether it was four steps or five to the bedroom; my father stood in the doorway and saw my grandmother. She was all aflame. She had got out of bed, somehow, and was standing in the middle of the room, next to the bed. The bed was burning, my grandmother's nightgown was burning, her stockings, her scarf, her hair, her face and her blue eyes; she was all ablaze and no longer screaming, the sky above the rooftops, the antennas, grey and smoky . . . She was, my father said later – he couldn't rightly say – but she was actually dancing as she burned,' says Sophie, not crying, with an embarrassed smile.

Bali Woman

At times winter reminds me of something. Of a mood I was once in, of a desire I once felt? I don't exactly know. It is cold. The air smells of smoke. Of snow. I turn around and listen for something I can't hear. There's a word on the tip of my tongue, I can't say it. A kind of restlessness, you know? You *do* know. But as you would say, whatever is nameless should remain nameless.

In any case, the night you didn't want to come along Christiane danced for me. She turned on the radio and danced to 'A Girl Like You', cheerleader face, flowing red hair. She was laughing, and she looked very beautiful. Markus Werner was wearing his grandmother's fur coat and a pair of household gloves made of pink rubber; the fur was mangy. 'You're so silly,' Christiane said. Markus Werner laid out the cocaine in short lines on his pocket mirror without looking at her. I wasn't tired. I sat on the sofa, leaning against him, his fur coat was wet with snow and smelled funny. I watched Christiane as she filled in the outlines of her mouth with a plum-coloured lipstick: her mouth was big and the lipstick was pointed, like a pen. Markus Werner looked up from his pocket mirror and stared into space.

Where were you? I had phoned you – you were sitting in front of your television set and you said you had taken the wrong drugs: you sounded tired and irritable, and you didn't want to come along. I said, 'Christiane has fallen in love.' You said, 'What else is new?' Then we were silent. I could hear small voices coming out of your television, sounds of war, an air-raid siren;

69

I knew it was cold in your room, frost flowers on the windows. You hung up.

The voice of Edwyn Collins sounded rough as ever. I smoked three cigarettes, one after the other. 'Who is it this time?' Markus Werner asked casually, his rubber gloves making a sticky sound. 'Oh, shut up,' said Christiane as she looked at herself sideways in the large mirror, one hand on her hip, gazing up from under her lashes; there were small blue shadows under her eyes, and she looked terrific. 'We're going to have fun,' she said, and kissed me on the mouth. I clutched Markus Werner's arm and whispered in his ear – apparently Christiane wasn't going to stop me – 'He's an important director. Really important, you know. He's married. We're going to his opening night party, there'll be food, vodka and everything, hey, we're going to have fun.' Christiane laughed and pulled me away from him.

Outside it was very cold. I thought of you in your room, sitting in your armchair in front of the television. I knew you wouldn't be watching any old film but sitting there in the semi-darkness, staring straight ahead; I was not disappointed, was not hurt, just a little sad perhaps. It was really cold. The air smelled of snow, and in the empty street our voices had such an unreal hollow sound that we stopped talking; the light from the streetlamps seemed frozen in place. Christiane in her high-heeled shoes fell down, and I looked at Markus Werner; we didn't help her to get up. At the intersection we took a taxi. 'To the theatre,' Christiane said. She sat down next to the driver, rolled down the window and turned on the radio. The driver made a face but didn't say anything.

Red flags were flying outside the theatre, and the doors were open. Markus Werner leaned forward and said, 'Now, about this play they did here this evening . . . ?' and Christiane gently warded him off. 'But what are you going to talk to him about if not the play?' said Markus Werner, giggling. Christiane drew his face close to hers and said very clearly, 'I don't want to *talk* with him at all. Understand?'

At the door I turned around once more. For one final time I considered going back, of going to your place and sitting down next to you in front of your television set. I would have turned off the television and looked at you: it could have been quite easy. I just couldn't make up my mind; then I took a deep breath and ran after Christiane and Markus Werner.

In the theater's Star Lounge long tables were set up. There was fabulous food and coolers full of vodka and small iced glasses, and they had engaged a Russian brass band and switched on the red lights. 'Now,' Christiane said, and disappeared. I got some bread and fish from the buffet, and Markus Werner stuffed vodka bottles and glasses into his coat pockets. He was still wearing those pink rubber gloves, but no one paid any attention to him. We sat down on the stairs and ate. I drank the vodka in great gulps and I began to feel warm, while Markus Werner sat there fidgeting and constantly wiping his nose. I said, 'You do too much coke,' and he said, 'Where is he, the great director?' The director was standing at the bar. He was tall and fat and seedy-looking, smoking a cigar and drinking whisky, he had this dissolute old-man sexiness that Christiane could never resist and he was famous. I pointed at him and said, 'That's him,' and Markus Werner began to laugh hysterically and said, 'Of course.' I looked at the director and thought of the countless directors and playwrights and actors and stage designers who had sat at mine and Christiane's kitchen table, had stood under our shower, had slept in our beds; I thought of their voices on our answering machine, their night-time banging on our door, the smashed glasses and unread letters; I thought that there was always something that wasn't quite enough, and this time, too, something wouldn't be enough; I thought of you, of the frost flowers, of the smell of smoke; I thought we're not enough either.

Christiane appeared. She must have been standing in front of a ladies' room mirror again because she had twisted her hair into this knot that I knew she would at some point undo by pulling out a single hairpin, allowing the hair to flow over her shoulders in a wave that made me feel weary. She made her appearance at the edge of the Star Lounge, wandering back and forth among the pillars for a while, approaching the bar then walking away again, lighting a cigarette and gazing about her from beneath lowered eyelids. The band was playing Ween's 'Buenas Tardes, Amigos'. Markus Werner wiped his nose on his rubber gloves, then wiped the gloves on his fur coat, saying, 'A real song of betrayal.' Christiane bobbed her head a little, buckled at the hip, swayed for an instant, then pushed her way onto the empty dance floor, to the dead centre, positioning herself on the big star, where the chandelier flooded her with red light. All this time the director had been staring vacantly at the dance floor, but now he turned away. When he turned back a little later, right away in fact, he looked at Christiane. And Christiane danced, cheerleader face, hands on her hips, threw her head back and seemed to be laughing; the slit in her dress went all the way up to her behind. Markus Werner giggled non-stop, though I didn't know whether it was because of the coke or Christiane's dancing. I had to laugh, and said, 'Hey, she knows how. She really knows how.'

She danced for a long time. At some point she raised her hand to her head and released the knot and her hair flooded down her back. Markus Werner buried his head between his knees and said, 'I can't stand it.' The director was one blurry, fat little heap of greed. I withdrew. I drank vodka and stared up into the lights of the chandelier, feeling a little dizzy, and I thought of all the nights we had got drunk together, you and I, at the wooden tables of some bar or other, it was always wintertime, always snowy outside, and it never grew light. I don't remember the summers. Why not? I've tried to understand why it's over between us, and I realized there was nothing to understand. I thought of you, of your room, of the blue light from the television set, the half-smoked cigarette in your left hand. I thought that you had known all this long before I did; you could have said something, something, anything.

Markus Werner nudged me and said, 'Look at that, hey, where are you? You've got to see this,' and I looked over at the dance floor. Christiane was still dancing and another woman was dancing with her. The woman was very small and slender. She looked like a child, a precocious child, her skin dark and her hair black. She wore a red dress, and when she spun in a circle you could see her naked buttocks and her pubic hair. She kept spinning, her small hands fluttering about her like birds. She was dancing barefoot, and her way of dancing was completely different from Christiane's. Christiane got out of step. She tried to use her cheerleader face, her swinging hips, the carefully calculated rhythmic movement of her legs, her coolness to counter the other woman's gentle movements, but it didn't work. She saw too much. The small woman had closed her eyes and seemed to be in another world, her black hair covering her face. Markus Werner stared open-mouthed; he lit a cigarette, like someone who has to concentrate, then turned abruptly towards me and asked matter-of-factly, 'Who's that?' And I said, 'That's his wife. The director's wife. She's from Bali. They got married in Bali.'

You would have liked her, this small woman. She was untouchable, in a way that you always liked, and was quite remote, and one could watch her and think up stories about her. She looked vulnerable and beautiful, with tiny, tiny feet, and she was so unreal in this lounge, on these marble tiles, under the light of the chandelier. Christiane left the dance floor and went to the bar. The director came over and stood next to her, not looking at his wife but at Christiane, who ordered a large glass of whisky. The small woman kept on dancing, and I knew that the stone floor under her feet was very cold. Markus Werner looked at me and said, 'Do you want to talk?' I said, 'No.' He got up and left. I went on drinking by myself. It was getting very late. I could see the snow through the large windows, thick, gently falling flakes. At some point Markus Werner was staggering around between the columns, quite drunk and holding – heaven knows where he got it – a megaphone; he kept shouting into the megaphone, always the same thing, but I couldn't understand a single word. I leaned my head against the banister and watched him. It occurred to me that I had never seen him in the daytime, and I wondered whether I wanted to know anything more about him other than the fact that he wore this fur coat in the winter and orange refuse collector jackets in the summer. Three times a week he went out with Christiane and me. I liked him; had I ever talked about him to anybody, I would actually have called him 'a friend'. Did I take him seriously? Did he take me seriously, did he want something when he said he wanted to talk with me, about what I wonder? I remembered that once he had said, in a very childlike manner, 'I could make a film about us.' I had said, 'What kind of film would it be?' He answered, 'A film about nothing happening, about nothing going on between us and around us, just a night like this with you and me and Christiane,' and I had laughed rather disparagingly. I watched him – he was much too young, high on coke and drunk, bellowing into his megaphone until his neck swelled. People were avoiding him. I felt sorry for him, and thought I never, ever wanted to see him again. I repressed the impulse to get up, walk over to him, take away the megaphone and kiss him. A girl was crouched on the star in the middle of the dance floor; she kept banging her head on the floor, her forehead was bloody, and she was crying and saying crazy things. The buffet was bare. On the big red sofa an actress was screwing a stagehand, the stagehand was sweating and the actress was desperately tearing at the back of his T-shirt, which had a picture of Mike Tyson biting Holyfield's ear. The small woman was gone, the director was gone, Christiane was gone. It was still snowing, and somebody was throwing glasses against the wall, and two unreal handicapped men in wheelchairs rolled across the dance floor and disappeared behind the columns. The actress pulled her skirt down, staggered up onto the small stage and said, 'For baby,' into an over-modulating microphone, she said, 'For baby, for baby,' then she collapsed. I closed my eyes. I heard Markus Werner yelling, but I still couldn't understand him. I fell asleep. I woke up again because Christiane was standing before me and pulling at my arm; she still looked as she had hours ago, in the apartment, on the street, in the taxi; she looked so wintry, so cool, so cold, her mouth frosty and thin-lipped. She shook me and said, 'Get up. We've got to go, we're going somewhere else, where's Werner, what are you doing here anyway?' She didn't say this quickly and agitatedly but very quietly and precisely. I got up and clung to her, looking into her eyes: her eyes were ice blue. I said, 'Christiane. How are things?' and she looked at me and said, 'Shitty. Things are shitty. But we're going there anyway now.'

Are you jealous? Just a tiny bit? A little curious and nervous – wondering where? Where are they going now? You would have gone home. No, you're not jealous, you never were. We went to look for Markus Werner and found him in the toilet, standing in front of the sink, rinsing something off his rubber gloves, and from one of the cubicles came a girl's whining voice, saying, 'What's wrong, why are you stopping now? I don't understand.' Christiane grimaced in disgust, kicked the cubicle door shut with her left foot, and Markus Werner turned around and said, much too softly, 'Does it have to be this way?' 'She's waiting,' Christiane said. 'She's waiting, and we have to go now, this minute,' and Markus Werner suddenly looked helpless and as though it was all too much for him and said pleadingly, 'Who's waiting? Who's waiting?' Christiane, already out in the hall, turned around annoyed and shouted, 'The Bali woman. The Bali woman is waiting.'

The clock outside the theatre had stopped at eleven. The snow had formed a deep layer on the street, on the cars, on the streetlamps, and the world was silent and roaring in my ears. The Bali woman, still barefoot and coatless in her red dress, was standing there next to a taxi, holding the door open for us. As Christiane pushed Markus Werner into the taxi his megaphone fell into the snow, then she pushed me in after him and then got in too. Markus Werner whispered, 'Your eyes break my heart, little sister.' I didn't know whose eyes he meant and wondered whether this was the sentence he had been yelling through the megaphone all evening. The Bali woman sat down on the seat next to the driver, turned around and smiled at us. I smiled back. As the taxi drove off, I leaned over to Christiane and said softly, 'So where to? Where are we going now?' and Christiane, looking out the window, said, 'To his place. Or hers. We're going to her apartment; he's already there, she wants us to come with her now.' I said, 'Why does she want that?' and Christiane shrugged. I asked, 'Why do you want to?' and she said, 'That's neither here nor there.'

The key to your apartment is on the ledge above the door. I know that. I could stand on tiptoe in the dark hallway, feel for it with my fingers and take it down, put it into the keyhole, quietly unlock the door. I could walk across the hall to your room: you would have turned off the television set by now and gone to sleep. I could stand next to your bed, watch you while you sleep, lie down next to you, you wouldn't notice a thing. But the key isn't lying there for me. I know that too. It's lying there for the one person we've never talked about, it's lying there, ready for her. When the time comes she'll get up on tiptoe, feel around for it, unlock the door, put her suitcases next to your bed and wake you. That's how it is, isn't it? You're waiting. You don't know her, this person, but you know she'll come, and that's what you're waiting for, sitting there and looking at the frost flowers and waiting. I am waiting too.

In any case the Bali woman had no key. She didn't have a key to her own apartment, or she pretended not to have one. We stood outside her apartment door, and she pressed her small brown thumb on the bell, and the bell rang shrilly. Markus Werner lolled around on the landing, wiping his nose, and said, exhausted, 'I can't go on.' The Bali woman turned around and smiled at him. Up to that point she hadn't said a single word, and I could see that her front teeth had been filed down to small stumps and were completely straight. Markus Werner gave her a strained smile and said with exaggerated precision, 'Perhaps we had better leave again?' and then the door opened and there, in the dark of the hallway, stood several small children, four or five tiny children in pyjamas, barefoot, with tousled hair. They stared at us, and we stared back. The children were a grotesque mixture of their parents, with the heavy spongy physicality of their father but eyes as dark, small and distinctive as their mother's. The Bali woman stepped forward into this swarm of pyjamas, stuffed animals and soft children's hands, and the children clung to her and spoke to her in a foreign language. Markus Werner looked at Christiane, 'Did you know about this?' And Christiane, for the first time at a loss, said, 'No, I didn't.'

In the hallway of the director's apartment we twice stepped on hamsters. The hamsters made ghastly noises, and the Bali woman laughed, picked them up, and threw them into one of the many rooms in the apartment. The children took a final peek through the crack in the door and then disappeared. The director was nowhere to be seen, and the apartment was dark. The Bali woman led us into the kitchen, lit candles, put water on to boil. Embarrassed, we sat down at the kitchen table; I wanted to sit next to Markus Werner, and Christiane wanted to sit next to me, and we kept moving around for a long time, our sense of shame obvious. Finally we were all seated. The kitchen was large and warm, and outside the windows it was night; unusual garlands were strung across the ceiling; there was a strange smell. We were silent. Christiane avoided my eyes. Like a child, Markus Werner whispered, 'What is it we're doing here?' and nobody answered him. The Bali woman made tea from green leaves, placing small cups, honey and sugar on the table. She poured with slow, confident movements, smiling all the time, finally sitting down next to Christiane. Markus Werner was looking at a photo hanging on the wall above the table. In it the director stood next to the Bali woman, and in the background were palm trees and a too-blue ocean; the director was naked except for a tiny loincloth and an ornament of bananas and flowers on his head. He was looking into the camera sidelong and obviously embarrassed, the Bali woman was holding his hand, wasn't smiling; the sky above them looked like rain. Markus Werner said, still with excessive precision, 'Your wedding?' and the Bali woman, who had just put her face very close to Christiane's, drew back and nodded. Christiane cleared her throat and put her hands on the table as though she were about to start a meeting. She said, in a determined and firm tone of voice, 'So where is he?' Markus Werner answered on behalf of the Bali woman, 'He's asleep already.'

I think we had some good winters together. Was it one or were there several? I don't remember anymore, and you'd say it wasn't important anyway. We had snow and crisp cold weather, and every time I said I really liked being cold you'd look at me as though you understood. We went for walks when the sun was shining. Those long shadows, and you would break icicles off the tree branches and suck on them. When you fell on the ice I laughed till the tears came to my eyes. We made no promises, and I too wanted it that way; still – forgive me – I am jealous of all the winters you're going to spend without me. I believe that from now on things will always be the way they were in that kitchen at that table sitting next to Markus Werner, with Christiane and the Bali woman. Morning came. I was so tired. I know that things were never any different, I just happened to have been wrong once.

The sky was turning pale outside the windows. It was snowing again, and the snow began to glow. Christiane stood up once, then sat down again. Markus Werner took off his rubber gloves and leaned against me. He kissed me quickly and softly on the neck. The Bali woman saw us and smiled. She said, 'There are many jokes in *Deutschland.*' Her voice sounded very bright and child-like, and she stretched out the words and couldn't pronounce the '*sch*' properly. Markus Werner didn't move. Christiane emitted a short dry laugh and said irritably, 'What?' The Bali woman moved closer to the table, no longer smiling. Very seriously she said, 'Jokes. I have learned them all.' Markus Werner closed his eyes and said gently, 'Why don't you tell us one?' The Bali woman looked up at the garland-decorated ceiling and said, 'What is the difference between a blonde and the *Titanic*?' We didn't say anything. She waited four, five seconds, then said, 'With the *Titanic* you know how many were on her.' We still didn't say anything. She looked at us as though she expected an explanation, a clarification of the joke; she looked terribly serious, and her eyes were opened wide. Markus Werner still had his eyes closed, but Christiane's face wore an expression of panic that made me laugh. The Bali woman leaned farther forward and said, 'What do you say to a blonde who falls down the cellar stairs?' Again she waited two, three seconds – she actually seemed to be counting – then she answered herself, 'Bring back some beer.' She said, 'Bring back some beer,' and all the while she looked with the utmost concentration at the table as though she were reading the words off it. Then she straightened up. She was now sitting ramrod straight and speaking as though the words had been drilled into her head, 'How do you bury a blonde?' and she didn't stop after that. She told one blonde joke after the other, ten, twenty, fifty dumb blonde jokes, and I stared at her, stared at her strange, concentrated, crazy face; at some point I no longer understood her at all. She kept speaking faster and faster, and would ask the question and give the answer, ask the question and give the answer without a pause. And then I noticed that Christiane – for how long? – was crying. Markus Werner's head slid off my shoulder into my lap. He was asleep, and his grandmother's mangy fur enfolded his surprisingly small face. I put my hand under his cheek and supported his head. I felt my heart beating. I felt good.

Then all was quiet. In one of the back rooms an alarm clock rang and a director woke up; outside it had grown light. The Bali woman was silent. She didn't look at all exhausted. She got up and pulled Markus Werner off me and he fell against her, then she gently brushed the coat off his shoulders and moved him over to the kitchen bench. She pushed him down on it, covered him with his coat, stroked his forehead with her small brown hand, then kissed him on the mouth. Christiane and I got up and put on our coats. At the kitchen door we turned around once more, and there she was, standing next to the bench in her red dress, looking at us, gravely and directly. She did not say another word, and at that point we left.

Outside it was still cold. An early-morning streetcar drove past us, blue sparks flying off the overhead lines. The city was still quiet and the light was so bright it made me squint. Christiane stopped and tied her hair together at the back of her neck, and I wondered whether I ought to touch her, but I didn't. Her face was all white, and her lips were blue. Then we started to walk, the snow crunching under our feet. I thought that if you had been sleeping you would just be waking up. You would wake up and see the frost flowers on your windows.

It is cold. The air smells of snow. Of smoke. Are you listening for something you can't hear, do you have a word on the tip of your tongue that you can't say? Are you restless? Did we meet – just once – and isn't that enough? I'm going to sleep now. Does winter sometimes remind you of something, you don't know – of what?

Hunter Tompson Music

The day something does finally happen after all is the Friday before Easter. Hunter comes back towards evening; he has bought canned soup, cigarettes and white bread at the deli, and picked up the cheapest whiskey at the liquor store; he's tired, a little shaky in the knees. He walks along 85th Street, the green plastic deli bag swinging against his knee; on the asphalt the last remnants of March snow are melting into grey, dirty streaks. It is cold and the neon sign on the Washington-Madison flickers an irresolute 'Hotel-Hotel' into the darkness.

Hunter pushes the big swinging door open with the palm of his hand, the warmth drawing him in and taking his breath away. There are black footprints on the green hotel carpet runner. He enters the dim foyer, where dark red silk-covered walls, soft leather-upholstered corner settees and large crystal chandeliers tell a tale of time irretrievably past; the silk is rippled, the leather corner settees are worn and sagging, the candelabra have lost their sparkling cut-glass pendants, and instead of twelve light bulbs in each there are only two. The Washington-Madison is no longer a hotel. It is a refuge, a poorhouse for old people, a last dilapidated stop before the end, a place of ghosts. It happens only rarely that an ordinary hotel guest mistakenly finds his way here. As long as no one dies the rooms are booked for months ahead; when someone dies the room stays empty for a while, only to receive the next old man or woman, for a year or two, or for four days or five.

*   *   *   **

Hunter shuffles over to the reception desk, where Leach, the hotel owner, is busy picking his nose and going through the personals in the *Daily News*. Hunter hates Leach. Everybody in the Washington-Madison hates Leach, except for old Miss Gil, who has chosen to offer him her feeble and scarred heart. Leach isn't interested in Miss Gil. Leach is interested in himself, in the *Daily News* personals – only the perverse ones, Hunter suspects – and in money. Hunter puts the green deli bag down on the worn reception desk, takes a deep breath, and says, 'Mail.'

Leach doesn't even look up. He says, 'No mail, Mr Tompson. Naturally, no mail.' Hunter feels his heart trip. It doesn't really trip, it just skips, it skips a beat and hesitates and then goes on beating after all, almost mercifully, as though it wanted to say – just a little joke. Hunter holds on to the counter with his left hand and says, 'Please, would you mind checking to see whether I have any mail.'

Leach looks up with the expression of someone who's been repeatedly interrupted during a tremendously important task by something tremendously unimportant, and he points with a weary, ritual gesture at the empty compartments behind him. 'Your box is Box Number 93, Mr Tompson. As you can see, it's empty. As empty as every other day.'

Hunter stares at the empty box, at all the other empty boxes above and below it; in Box 45 there's Mr Friedman's chess magazine, and in Box 107 the knitting instructions for Miss Wenders. An unusually large number of knitting instructions. 'It looks as though Miss Wenders hasn't picked up her mail for several days, Mr Leach,' Hunter says. 'Maybe you should check to see if she's all right.'

Leach doesn't answer. Hunter, with a dull feeling of triumph, picks up his plastic bag from the desk and takes the elevator to the fourth floor. The elevator rumbles alarmingly, its routine maintenance is long overdue; at his floor the doors slide open, shaking and creaking. The hall light isn't working. Hunter gropes his way along the wall; ever since Mr Wright died three weeks ago in Room 95, the room across the hall, he has been alone in this corner of the fourth floor, and he is afraid. The red EXIT sign over the door to the stairway glows weakly. From the bathroom at the end of the hall come sounds of running water, violent nose-blowing and coughing. Hunter shudders. He washes himself as best he can at the sink in his room, and uses the communal bath with the big old tub as rarely as possible; sad to say, he finds old people for the most part disgusting.

Hunter turns the key in the lock, switches the light on, locks the door behind him. He unpacks the groceries, lies down on the bed, closes his eyes. Tiny green dots dance up and down in the blackness behind his closed eyelids. The building moves. It is always moving. The floors above him creak, somewhere a door slams, the elevator rumbles in the distance. Hunter can hear soft radio music, a telephone rings, something falls down with a dull thud, the sound of taxi horns rises from the street below. Hunter likes these noises. He likes the Washington-Madison in a certain sad, resigned way. He likes his room, for which he pays four hundred dollars a month; he replaced the twenty-watt bulb in the ceiling fixture with a sixty-watt bulb and put up blue curtains at the windows. He has arranged his books on the bookshelf, the tape recorder and tapes on the bureau, and hung two photographs above the bed. There's a chair for visitors who never come, and a telephone that never rings. Next to the sink a refrigerator, and on the refrigerator a hotplate. All the rooms are furnished like this. Once a week the bed linen is changed; when he moved in Hunter had insisted on doing it himself. He doesn't like the idea of the chambermaid rummaging around among his books, papers and tapes.

Hunter turns over on his back, pushes aside the curtain at the window next to the bed, and stares out; the grating of the fire escape stairway slices the dark sky into small squares. He falls asleep, then wakes up again and sits on the edge of the bed, glancing briefly at the brown, patterned rug between his feet. Then he gets up. It's going to snow one more time this March, he can feel it in his bones, a chilly, unpleasant prickling. But his tiredness is gone: the room is warm, there's banging in the heating pipes, and far away at the end of the hall Miss Gil is singing to herself in a thin, high voice. Hunter smiles briefly. He heats a can of soup on the hotplate, pours himself a glass of whiskey, and eats in front of the television. The newscaster on CNN reports in an apathetic voice that in East New York, Brooklyn, a boy shot three employees in a McDonald's. The boy appears on the television screen. He is black, and maybe seventeen years old; three police officers parade him before the cameras. A voice from nowhere asks about his motive. The boy looks directly into the cameras, he seems completely normal. He explains that he had ordered a Big Mac without pickles. Specifically without pickles. But he'd gotten a Big Mac *with* pickles.

Hunter turns off the television. In the hall the door to Room 95 slams shut. Hunter turns his head and listens, irritated; there is silence. He washes his plates and pot, pours himself another glass of whiskey, and stands in front of his tapes, undecided. Time for music. Time for music just like every other evening, time for a cigarette, time for time. What else should he do if not listen to music. Hunter rubs a hand over his eyes and briefly feels for his heartbeat. His heart is beating quietly and sluggishly. Maybe

Mozart. Or better still, Beethoven. Schubert as always is too sad. Bach. Johann Sebastian Bach, *The Well-Tempered Clavier, Book 1*. Hunter slides the cassette into the player and pushes the start button. There is a soft hissing sound. He sits down on the chair by the window and lights a cigarette.

Glenn Gould's playing is slow, concentrated and sustained. Now and then Hunter can hear him singing along softly, sometimes breathing heavily: Hunter likes that, he sees it as a personal touch. He sits on the chair, listening. He can either think well or not think at all while listening to music; either way it's nice. Taxi horns honk in the distance. Miss Gil has stopped singing, or perhaps Glenn Gould is louder than Miss Gil. Outside Hunter's door a floorboard creaks. The board creaks noisily. The board had always creaked noisily whenever Mr Wright would stand outside his door, wanting cigarettes or whiskey or company. Mr Wright is dead. He died three weeks ago, the only person ever to stand in front of Hunter's door.

Hunter stares at the door with wide-open eyes. The doorknob, unlike in the movies, does not turn, but there comes another creak. Hunter's heart suddenly starts beating surprisingly fast. New York is a crime-ridden city. Nobody would take him seriously if he were to shout for help. Leach would pretend he'd forgotten the police emergency number. Hunter gets up. He tiptoes to the door, his heart now skipping beats. He puts his hand on the doorknob, takes a deep breath, and flings open the door.

The girl stands in the red light of the EXIT sign. Hunter sees very small feet with curled toes, a mosquito bite scratched open on the left ankle, a tiny bit of dirt under the big toenail. Her bathrobe is frayed at the hem, blue with white appliquéd rabbits on the pockets. She has tied the robe very tightly around her waist, and under her arm she has a towel and a bottle of shampoo. With her right hand she holds the bathrobe closed at her throat: her lips are thin and she seems agitated. Water drips steadily from her wet hair onto the brown hall carpet. She squints and peers past Hunter into his room. Below her left eye there's a small birthmark. Involuntarily Hunter looks down at himself and notices that he can't see his belt buckle because his belly protrudes above it. The girl says something like, 'The music.'

Hunter pulls the door toward him and tries to block her view of the room. He can hear Miss Gil singing again, she's singing, *Honey pie, you are making me crazy,* and for some reason he finds this embarrassing. The girl says something like, 'Excuse me, the music,' pronouncing the words awkwardly and like a child, at the same time rubbing the toes of her right foot against her left calf.

Hunter gets goosepimples. He steps out into the hall and pulls the door shut behind him, saying, 'What do you mean?' The girl draws back and screws up her thin lips. Hunter feels his hand trembling on the doorknob. The girl, transferring the towel and shampoo bottle from her right arm to the left, says, 'Are you watching television or are you listening to music?' Hunter stares at her. He has a vague memory of some television show he has seen, but he doesn't understand her; she's speaking in a code but he can't crack the code: does he watch television or does he listen to music. What does that mean?

She says, 'Television or music? Commercial – advertisement – or really music?

Hunter repeats hesitantly, 'Really music,' and the girl, impatient now, bounces up and down on her toes and says, 'Bach.'

Hunter says, 'Yes, Bach. *The Well-Tempered Clavier,* Glenn Gould.'

She says, 'Well then. So you are listening to music.'

Hunter takes a deep breath, feeling his belly distending even more, but he immediately feels better. Of course he's listening to music. He wants to go back to the beginning, to the first question, and has difficulty hiding his confusion from her: he suspects she sees him as an old fool. He repeats, this time with more self-assurance, 'What do you mean?' The girl answers slowly, in the voice of a teacher whose pupil has finally understood, 'I stopped in front of the door to your room to listen to the music.'

Hunter smiles uncomprehendingly, thinks of dogs baring their teeth. Miss Gil sings *I'm in love but I'm lazy,* and he feels an urge to wring her wrinkled neck, as they do to ducks in the comics. He giggles. The girl giggles too, and says, 'She's lost some of her marbles, hasn't she?' Hunter stops giggling and says gruffly, 'She's old.'

The girl raises her left eyebrow. Hunter turns the doorknob, ready to retreat to his room, and says self-consciously, 'Yes, well.'

Taking a resolute breath and shifting from one foot to the other, the girl says three sentences in a row. Hunter has to make a tremendous effort to concentrate. She says, 'You know, I'm here only temporarily. Room 95. It was nice to hear your music; you see, they swiped my cassette player.'

Before she's even finished saying 'cassette player' Hunter says, 'Who?' He feels he has to gain time: this is all too much for him, she is much too young for this hotel, she talks so funny. She says, 'These guys at Grand Central, they swiped my backpack and my cassette player and all my tapes, and now I can't listen to music any more. That's bad. Nothing works without music.' She looks at Hunter expectantly and attentively.

Hunter says, 'I'm sorry to hear that,' and peers down the dark hallway looking for help. Miss Gil has stopped singing, and he has a faint hope that she'll come to the elevator and interrupt this situation. Miss Gil doesn't come. The girl – Hunter senses that she is observing him – says with peculiar emphasis, 'Do you live here?' Hunter turns to face her again. The expression around her mouth is almost cruel, and her upper body is bent forward possessively; water is still dripping from her hair.

'Yes,' says Hunter. 'I mean, I . . .' He breaks off in mid-sentence and is briefly tempted to leave her standing there, to go back into his room and slam the door in her face.

'This is a peculiar hotel, isn't it?' the girl asks, one of her hands now in the pocket of her bathrobe, causing the rabbit appliqué to bulge obscenely. Hunter feels totally exhausted. He longs for Glenn Gould, for the blue curtains of his room, for sleep. He is no longer accustomed to this sort of thing; he is no longer accustomed to meeting people, to having conversations. He says, 'Excuse me,' and the girl sighs dramatically. She takes her room key out of her bathrobe pocket and smiles reassuringly at Hunter. 'Shall we go out for supper together? Perhaps tomorrow evening, you could take me to a good restaurant and tell me something about the city, you know what I mean.' Hunter remembers that he hasn't eaten out for years, that he doesn't know any good restaurants, that he can't tell her anything about the city, that he knows nothing at all. He says, 'Of course, with pleasure' – he would have said, 'Of course, with pleasure,' to anything – and the girl grins and says, 'Well then, tomorrow evening at eight; I'll pick you up. Goodnight.'

Hunter nods. He watches her back as she unlocks her door, the terry-towelling of her bathrobe wet and dark along her spine. He looks at her closed door and hears her humming behind it, brushing her teeth. He sees the light under the door go out. He is not sure he'll have the strength to go back into his room.

The next morning he wakes up because in the hall outside the communal bathroom Miss Gil is arguing with Mr Dobrian. Miss Gil's high, shrill voice breaks into his room, her voice is shaking and sounds triumphant. 'You pig!' Miss Gil yells. 'You pig, you filthy peeping Tom, you scoundrel! To come bursting into the bathroom when women are washing themselves; I'm going to tell Mr Leach!' Hunter hears Mr Dobrian's fragile, tired, old-man's voice, 'But you purposely leave the door unlocked, Miss Gil; if you would lock it this couldn't happen!' It was the same every day. Miss Gil never locked the door; someone would go in, see her standing there naked, wrinkled, and shrivelled, leave again in disgust, then have to endure her endless ranting. Hunter sighs and pulls the blanket over his head, sleep slipping away from him like a cloth, the face of the girl with the wet hair appearing briefly before him. He thinks of their date, of having supper with her that evening, and feels an ache in his stomach. He shouldn't have done it. He shouldn't have agreed to it. He doesn't know what to talk about with her; she seems a bit naïve, and it's been a long time since he has had any thoughts about women. What a crazy idea, to think of going out with a stranger, a girl much too young for him, and in his condition no less; a grotesque, a ridiculous idea.

Hunter sits up. He looks briefly through the window at the sky, which is grey and overcast. Easter Saturday, a free day, a terribly free evening. Miss Gil's voice, still nagging, is moving farther down the hall. Hunter gets up, washes, dresses, pulls open the window and stares briefly down at the wet, early-morning street. A fat child carrying a box under his arm trips and falls, gets up again, walks on. Hunter takes the elevator to the ground floor, hurries to reach the front door, hurries to escape Leach's voice, but is too slow.

'Mr Tompson!' Leach's voice is both enticing and offensive. Hunter stops in mid-stride and turns halfway toward the reception desk. He doesn't answer.

'Have you seen her already, Mr Tompson?'

'Have I seen whom already?' says Hunter.

'The girl, Mr Tompson. The girl I put into Room 95 for you!' Leach succeeds in placing such a loathsome emphasis on the word 'girl' that a cold shiver runs down Hunter's back.

'No,' he says, his hand already on the glass pane of the swinging door. 'I haven't seen her yet.' Leach triumphantly calls after him, 'Oh, but you're lying, Mr Tompson! She herself told me this morning that she talked with you. She was very impressed, Mr Tompson!'

Hunter lets the swinging door slam shut, steps out into the cool street air and spits. The girl seems to be more stupid than he thought. He walks along 85th Street to Broadway. Even though it's Saturday and early morning, there's already heavy traffic. The traffic lights flash green and red, and crowds stream out of the stores. A nightmarish giant Easter rabbit stands on the corner of 75th and throws chocolate eggs into the crowd. Hunter walks around aimlessly, absorbed in his own thoughts; the sky is heavy with rain and there's an icy crackling in the air. People bump into him; at the corner of Broadway and 65th he stands around for five minutes until the newspaper vendor points out to him that the light has just turned green for the third time. He turns and starts walking uptown again, heading toward the park, and buys a sandwich and a take-away coffee at a little coffee shop. A tattered beggar approaches people and tugs at their shopping bags. Hunter steers clear of him but bumps into an enormously fat black woman. He excuses himself, and she smiles and says, 'It's nothing, honey.' The crazy man in front of Filene's Basement yells, 'Too much electricity!' He's been standing there as long as Hunter can remember, yelling, 'Too much electricity makes people crazy!' Passers-by laugh and throw dimes at his feet, but he never picks them up. Outside Zabar's some workers eat salads out of plastic containers, sitting next to each other, their feet equal distances apart. Hunter turns into a side street. It's quieter here, green wreaths with yellow ribbons hang on the front doors of four-storey brick town houses. In the park he sits down to drink the coffee, cold by now, and eat the sandwich. The day glides by. Towards noon a gentle rain begins to fall.

Hunter continues to sit there. Pigeons peck at rat-poison-yellow grains, a girl on rollerblades whizzes by, black nannies holding the hands of sickly and haughty-looking white children sit down next to him. Hunter's eyes remain fixed on the pebbles between his feet, grey pebbles with white dots. He feels an uneasiness in his joints, in his hands, he has never felt before. It is an uneasiness that has nothing to do with the snow, although yesterday's chilly prickling has increased. The park, which usually makes him feel calm and tired, today seems inaccessible, unfriendly. An old Asian woman pokes around in the garbage cans with a wire coat hanger, babbling to herself, before, morosely and without any booty, disappearing among the trees on the other side of the lawn. In front of Hunter's bench a pigeon keels over, claws twitching, then is still. Hunter moves to the next bench. The clouds part, revealing a pale, dull March sky. Perplexed, he thinks, 'Time. And time,' and then he thinks about nothing. He leaves the park as long shadows stretch out between the benches and walks back to Broadway, the evening traffic just as idiotically heavy as in the morning. He turns into 83rd Street, the indoor garage near the corner recklessly spits out cars. Hunter crosses to the other side of the street, and feeling cold thrusts his hands deeper into his coat pockets. There's a light on in Lenny's store.

Hunter carefully pushes the small glass door open. He gets tangled up in the felt curtain behind it and trips in the dark. He can hear Lenny laughing softly. He disentangles himself from the curtain and laughs too, much against his will; Lenny is sitting in his dusty rocking chair behind the cash register holding his hand in front of his mouth like a girl. 'Stop that,' Hunter says. Lenny, exaggerating, takes a deep breath, and disappears as he reaches down to a shelf below the cash register. He reappears with a bottle of whiskey and two glasses. It is warm in the store. Filaments of dust flicker in the yellow light, and there is a smell of paper and damp wood. Lenny's rocking chair among books, picture frames, Halloween masks, mouldy little boxes and bolts of fabric, plastic flowers, canned food, yellowed postcards. Umbrellas, wigs, baseball bats. Hunter brushes a stack of ancient lottery tickets off a garden chair and sits down. Lenny pours the whiskey; dust seems to have settled in the folds of his face, and the eyes behind his thick lenses have a moist gleam. He says, 'You were here only the day before yesterday, Tompson.' Hunter smiles and says, 'I'm leaving right away.' Lenny doesn't answer and rocks his chair back into the darkness of the store. The whiskey tastes salty. Somewhere water is dripping; the noises of the street are far away. Hunter is beginning to feel warm. He no longer knows why he's here. He no longer wants to know why he's here, he just wants to keep on sitting here the way he always sits here: quietly, for a long time, without a reason, then leave. Lenny, watching him, senses this. Lenny is clever. He clears his throat, spits the mucus into an old tin bowl, and says, 'Tompson. You don't mean you actually want to buy something, do you?'

Hunter sits up straight. The garden chair creaks, and he can hear the blood roaring in his ears. He says, 'I need a cassette player. Nothing special, just one of those little portable ones, I thought maybe you'd have something like that.' He tries to give his voice a casual, carefree note. Behind his glasses Lenny's eyes become small, narrow slits. 'But you already have a cassette player, Tompson. Why do you need another one?'

Hunter clears his throat. He would like to evade Lenny's gaze, and already regrets having asked at all; he is unable to lie. He says, 'I want to give it as a present.' Lenny looks away. He rocks back and forth, slowly, idly, whistling briefly to himself, shaking his head. Hunter breathes carefully. Lenny gets up and disappears in the depths of the store. Glass shatters, books fall, dust rises. Lenny coughs and curses, tugs at something, comes back; in his knotty, brown-flecked hands he holds a small, almost dainty tape recorder with a silver cassette deck.

Hunter is perspiring. The collar of his winter coat chafes his neck and the wool scarf itches. Hunter finds it's unbearably hot. Lenny puts the cassette recorder next to the cash register and busies himself wiping it with a dust rag. He looks concerned. He actually looks concerned. Hunter turns his head away and moves his garden chair back into the murky twilight. Lenny leans forward and says, 'You know that I don't sell things anymore. I just sit here. I don't sell anything anymore.'

'Yes,' Hunter says weakly. 'I know.'

Lenny sighs indulgently, spits again, then chortles softly. 'I'm surprised at you, Tompson. I'm really surprised. I guess you're not planning to give this recorder to Leach. Or to Miss Gil.' He eyes Hunter through his thick lenses, a dust flake quivering on his bald head. 'Now, Tompson. Who's this recorder supposed to be for?' Hunter makes no reply. He feels the weariness unfolding between his shoulder blades and wipes the sweat from his forehead with the back of his hand. Lenny comes out from behind the cash register, kicks over two piles of books, and puts the little recorder in Hunter's lap. He says, 'Take it. I don't need it any more. If you change your mind, bring it back. Tompson . . .' Lenny breaks off and shuffles back to the rocking chair. He sits down and looks at his spit in the tin bowl. Hunter touches the silver tape deck. It is cool and smooth. He wishes Lenny would say something else. He wishes Lenny would take the recorder back again, he wishes he were back in his room, in his bed, in the darkness. Lenny is silent. Water is dripping. Somewhere paper rustles. Hunter gets up, takes the cassette recorder and goes to the door. He says, 'Thanks a lot.' 'It's nothing,' says Lenny from the depth of his rocking chair, Hunter stands there with his back to him, waiting, feeling his heart beating. Lenny says, 'Tompson?' Hunter clears his throat. Lenny says, 'Will you come again, tomorrow, the day after tomorrow?' Hunter says, 'Sure.' He pushes the felt curtain aside, opens the small glass door and smells the snow. 'I hope so,' Lenny says, as Hunter steps out into the cold, dark street.

At the Washington-Madison Leach is sitting behind the reception desk, reading the *Daily News*. He doesn't look up. Hunter, the recorder concealed under his coat, takes the elevator up, tiptoes through the hall, unlocks the door to his room and locks it behind him. His knees are shaking. It is 6.45. It is quiet in the hallway and in Room 95.

An hour. Another hour, then she will come. Hunter sits on the chair by the window and stares at his closet. He has wrapped the cassette player in newspaper and tied a woollen thread around it. It's now on the table, and it looks ridiculous. Hunter turns away, then goes over to the closet and takes out a suit. It is black and smells of dust, worn at the knees and elbows, the collar shiny.

The last time he wore the suit was to Mr Wright's funeral, it's his Washington-Madison funeral suit, and the thought that he's going to wear it tonight makes Hunter explode in hysterical laughter. He feels sick. He feels sick to his stomach, around his heart, and in his throat; he throws the suit on the bed and runs hot water into the sink. The girl isn't going to make him wash in the communal bathroom. The girl won't make him wash at all, he'll just shave and comb his hair; it's all hopeless anyway. In front of the mirror above the sink Hunter opens his eyes very slowly. The mirror is small, misted over with steam, Hunter looks at his face in the merciful white steam. He shaves carefully, but his hands are shaking too much. He cuts his chin slightly, causing some blood to ooze out, its colour a strange, sickly red. Hunter gags. He takes a deep breath, runs cold water over his wrists, counts. He can smell the shaving foam, the soap, peppermint. He staunches the blood with a small scrap of newspaper, puts on his suit; the sleeves are too short, a button is missing. Hunter feels as though he is in a dream. Sleepwalking. Almost apathetic. He lights a cigarette, hitches up his trousers, and sits down on the edge of the bed. He coughs. It's 7.45. He waits.

The square of sky between the grating of the fire escape turns pale, then black. It's raining a little. The clock on his night table is ticking, and the water gurgles in the heating pipes. For a moment the building lurches in a strange unaccustomed motion. 'Like a ship,' Hunter thinks. 'Like a ship, it has cast off, has left shore a long time ago, I just didn't notice.' All the sounds, as though coming from far away. The hand of the clock wanders in a circle, drawing the hours and hours. The girl is not coming, of course she's not coming. Hunter lies on his bed and smiles, looks up at the ceiling, water stains up there, cracks in the plaster – disappointed relief. After all, what would it have been like? What would it have looked like, this evening in a good restaurant, the mocking smiles of the waiters, the coins in his pocket, his trembling hands, his difficulties swallowing. She would have had to do the talking. He would have been unable to speak, would only have listened to the beating of his heart, the heartbeats getting faster and faster, until . . . Hunter lies on his bed and smiles. 'Time,' he thinks. 'Time and time.' The clock says eleven. He pulls the blanket up over his knees and rolls over on his side, his gaze touching the objects in the room, their worn, soft familiarity. It is warm. His tiredness is heavy and pleasant.

Around midnight the door to Room 95 slams shut. Hunter hadn't heard the girl, her light springy step in the dark hall, a sound probably too unfamiliar. He sits up and listens, everything remains still. He gets up, feels dizzy, and things go black before his eyes, then it passes. He takes his suit off again, the jacket, the trousers, wrinkled now and crumpled, carefully hangs them up in the closet. He stands in front of his cassettes, Mozart and Bach, sad Schubert and soft, gentle Satie. The Portuguese fado songs for Sundays and the voice of Janis Joplin for which he is too old, has always been too old. Sometimes, in an upbeat mood, Astor Piazolla. And that American, that big, crazy, ugly bird from California whose 'Jersey Girl' is the only song he has ever heard him sing, but he had loved it. And again Mozart and Schumann, between them a recording by Stevens, where did that come from? Hunter slides his hand over the cassette cases, shakes his head, smiles, confused. Tango music. Callas arias. Music and time, time, *Die Winterreise*, the strange African songs he bought at the flea market in Tompkins Square seven years ago, or was it eight or ten? Hunter doesn't cry. He turns the cassette cases over in his hands. He can't read his own writing any more, jazz and poetry, the voice of Truman Capote. Then he packs them up, getting a small shoebox out of the closet, putting the cassette cases into it, very neatly, side by side; some have no writing on them, let her find out for herself. Also the Glenn Gould cassette that was in the player. That one too, Hunter forgets nothing. The girl knocks on the door, it's already late, so late, so late. Hunter puts the cover on the shoebox and places the box on top of the little package containing the cassette player. He opens the door a crack and slides both out into the hall.

The girl says, 'Please.' She wedges her foot into the door. Hunter pushes it back with both hands, says, 'Happy Easter,' and pushes the door shut. The girl, on the other side of the door, says, 'Please,' once more, says, 'I'm sorry. I know. I'm much too late.' Hunter squats on the floor and doesn't answer. He can hear her breathe. He can hear her pick up the two small boxes, lift the cover off the shoebox, tear the newspaper off the little package. She says, 'Oh.' The cassette cases clatter softly against each other, she says, 'Good heavens,' then starts to cry. Hunter puts his hands over his face and presses his thumbs on his closed eyelids till there's an explosion of colour. The girl in the hall cries. Maybe she's vain. Maybe she's disappointed. Hunter leans his head against the door. His head is so heavy, and he doesn't want to hear anymore, but he hears anyway. The girl says, 'You shouldn't have done this.' Hunter says, very softly – he doesn't know if she can hear him, but after all he is speaking to himself – 'I know. But that's the way I want it.' The girl says, 'Thank you.' Hunter nods. He hears her coat rustle; it's probably a plastic coat, maybe green. She pushes against the door, but it does not yield. She asks, 'You won't open it just one more time?' Hunter shakes his head. She says, 'Just one question, one last question, would you answer one question?' 'Yes,' Hunter says, uttering it into the crack between the door and the wall; he guesses her mouth is somewhere around there, her thin-lipped, nervous, restless mouth. She says, 'I only want to know why you live here, why, would you tell me that?' Hunter places his face against the crack: there's a little draught, and cold air enters, coolness. He closes his eyes again, says, 'Because I can leave. Pack my suitcases, any day, any morning, pull the door shut behind me, go.' The girl is silent. Then she says, 'Go where, though?' Hunter instantly replies, 'That's a totally irrelevant question.' The pressure against the door subsides. The plastic coat rustles. The girl seems to be getting up, the cool draught from the crack is gone. 'Yes,' she says. 'I understand. Goodnight.' 'Goodnight,' Hunter says; he knows she will have finished packing her suitcase, the cassette player, his music and will have left before it's light outside.

The Summer House, Later

Stein found the house in the winter. He phoned me sometime early in December and said, 'Hello,' then nothing. I didn't say anything either. He said, 'This is Stein.' I said, 'I know.' He said, 'So, how's it going?' I said, 'Why are you calling?' He said, 'I've found it.' Not understanding, I asked him, 'What did you find?' and he answered irritably, 'The house! I found the house.'

The house. I remembered. Stein and his talk about *the* house, away from Berlin, a country house, a manor house, an estate house, linden trees in front, chestnuts at the back, sky above, a Brandenburg lake, at least two and a half acres of land, maps spread out, marked up, driving around for weeks in the area, searching. Then when he came back he looked peculiar, and the others said, 'What's he talking about? Nothing's ever going to come of this.' I forgot about it when I no longer saw Stein. Just as I forgot about him.

As always when Stein somehow surfaced and I couldn't think of much to say, I automatically lit a cigarette. I said hesitantly, 'Stein? Did you buy it?' and he shouted, 'Yes!' and then he dropped the telephone. I had never heard him shout before. And then he was back on the line, and kept shouting, shouted, 'You *have* to see it, it's incredible, it's great, it's terrific!' I didn't ask why I, of all people, ought to see it. I kept listening, even though for a long while he said nothing more.

'What are you doing right now?' he finally asked. It sounded downright obscene, and his voice trembled slightly. 'Nothing,' I said. 'I'm just sitting around reading the paper.' 'I'll pick you up. In ten minutes,' Stein said and hung up.

Five minutes later he was here. He didn't take his thumb off the bell even after I had opened the door. I said, 'Stein, this is getting on my nerves. Stop ringing.' I wanted to say, Stein, it's freezing outside, I don't feel like driving out there with you, get lost. Stein stopped ringing the bell, tilted his head, wanted to say something, said nothing. I got dressed. We drove off. His taxi smelled of cigarettes. I rolled down the window and turned my face toward the cold air.

At that time my relationship with Stein, as the others referred to it, had already been over for two years. It hadn't lasted long and consisted mainly of trips we took together in his taxi. I had met him in his taxi. He'd driven me to a party, and on the autobahn expressway he had pushed a Trans Am cassette into the tape player; when we arrived I told him the party must be somewhere else, and we drove on, and at some point he switched off the meter. He came home with me, put his plastic bags down in my hall and stayed for three weeks. Stein had never had an apartment of his own, but moved around the city with these plastic bags, sleeping now here and now there, and when he couldn't find anything he slept in his taxi. He wasn't what one thinks of as a homeless person. He was clean, well dressed, never seedy, and he had money because he was working. He just didn't have his own apartment. Maybe he didn't want one.

During the three weeks Stein lived at my place we drove around the city in his taxi. The first time we went down Frankfurter Allee to where it ends and back again, listening to Massive Attack and smoking. We drove up and down Frankfurter Allee for probably an hour, till Stein said, 'Do you understand?'

My head was completely empty. I felt hollowed out and in a strange state of suspended animation. The street ahead of us was broad and wet from the rain, the wipers moved across the windshield, back and forth. The Stalin-era buildings on both sides of the street were huge and strange and beautiful. The city was no longer the city I knew, but was autarkical and deserted. Stein said, 'Like a giant prehistoric animal.' I said I understood, I had stopped thinking.

After that we nearly always spent our time driving around in his taxi. For every route Stein had a different kind of music, Ween for country roads, David Bowie for downtown, Bach for the avenues, Trans Am only for the autobahn. We almost always drove on the autobahn. When the first snow fell, Stein would get out of the car at every rest stop, run to a snow-covered field and perform slow and concentrated Tae Kwon Do movements until, laughing and furious, I shouted for him to come back. I wanted to drive on, I was cold.

At some point I had had enough. I packed his three plastic bags and said it was time for him to find a new place to stay. He thanked me and left. He moved in with Christiane, who lived on the floor below me, then with Anna, then Henrietta, then Falk, then with the others. He screwed them all, that was unavoidable; he was pretty good-looking. Fassbinder would have been delighted with him. He was there with us, and yet also not there. He didn't belong, but for one reason or another he stayed. He posed as a model in Falk's studio, laid cable for Anna's concerts, listened to Heinze's readings at the Red Salon. He applauded when we applauded in the theatre, drank when we drank, did drugs when we did. He was there at our parties, and in the summer he came along when we drove out to the shabby, lopsided little country houses, which everyone had before long, and on whose rotting fences someone had scrawled *'Berliner raus!'* And now and then one of us would take him to bed with us, and now and then one of us watched.

Not me. I didn't repeat. Frankly – it wasn't my kind of thing. Nor could I remember what it was like – that is, what sex with Stein had been like.

We sat around with him, there in the gardens and houses of people we had nothing to do with. Workers had lived there, small farmers, and amateur gardeners who hated us and whom we hated. We avoided the locals; just thinking about them ruined everything. It wasn't right. We robbed them of this feeling they had of being among themselves, and we disfigured the villages, the fields, and even the sky; they picked that up from the way we strode around in our Easy Rider gait, flicked our burnt-down roaches into the flower beds in their front yards, the way we nudged each other excitedly. But we wanted to be there regardless. Inside the houses we tore down wallpaper, removed rubber and plastic; Stein did that. We sat in the garden, drank wine, gazed idiotically at Tree Clump Circled by Swarm of Gnats, and talked about Castorf and Heiner Müller and Wawerzinek's latest flop at the Volksbühne Theatre. When Stein had finished he sat down with us. He had nothing to say. We did LSD, and so did Stein. Toddi staggered into the evening light, drivelling something about 'blue' every time he touched anything. Stein smiled with exaggerated cheerfulness and said nothing. He couldn't get the knack of our sophisticated, neurasthenic, fucked-up look, even though he tried; mostly he watched us as though we were actors performing on a stage. Once, I was alone with him, I think it was in the garden of Heinze's house in Lunow, the others having set off for the sunset on speed. Stein was putting away glasses, ashtrays, bottles, and chairs. Soon he was done and there was nothing left to remind us of the others. 'Do you want some wine?' he asked. I said, 'Yes.' We drank and smoked in silence, and he smiled every time our eyes met. And that was it.

I thought, 'And that was it,' as I now sat next to Stein in the taxi, on Frankfurter Allee heading toward Prenzlau in the afternoon traffic. The day was hazy and cold, with dust in the air, goggle-eyed, stupid, tired drivers next to us giving us the finger. I smoked a cigarette and wondered why I of all people had to be sitting next to Stein now. Why of all people he had called me – was it because I had been a beginning for him? Because he couldn't reach Anna or Christiane or Toddi? Because none of them would have driven out there with him? And why was I driving out there with him? I couldn't come close to an answer. I threw the cigarette end out of the window, ignoring the comments of the driver next to us; it was awfully cold in the taxi. 'Is something wrong with the heater, Stein?' Stein didn't answer. It was the first time just the two of us sat in his car since back then. Indulgently I said, 'Stein, what kind of house is it? What did you pay for it?' Stein looked absent-mindedly into the rear-view mirror, drove through red lights, changed lanes incessantly, drawing on his cigarette until the glowing end reached his lips. He said, 'Eighty thousand. I paid eighty thousand marks for it. It's beautiful. I took one look and I knew – this is it.' He had red spots on his face and kept pounding on the horn with the flat of his hand as he pulled ahead of a bus that had the right of way. I said, 'Where did you get eighty thousand marks?' He glanced at me briefly and answered, 'You're asking the wrong questions.' I decided not to say any more.

*   *   *

We left Berlin. Stein drove off the autobahn and onto a country road. It began to snow. I felt tired, as I always do riding in cars. I stared at the windshield wipers, into the whirling snow coming toward us in concentric circles, and thought about driving with Stein two years ago, about the odd euphoria, about the indifference, about the strangeness. He was driving more calmly, glancing at me every now and then. I asked, 'Doesn't the tape deck work anymore?' He smiled, said, 'Oh sure. I didn't know ... whether you'd still like it.' I rolled my eyes. 'Of course I do,' and pushed the Callas cassette – the one on which Stein had recorded a montage of a Donizetti aria repeated twenty times in succession – into the tape deck. He laughed. 'You still remember.' Callas sang, her voice rising and falling, and Stein sped up and slowed down. I had to laugh, too, and I briefly touched his cheek. His skin was unusually bristly. I wondered, 'What's usual?' Stein said, 'See.' I saw that he immediately regretted it.

After Angermünde he turned off the road, stopping in front of a driveway that led to a low building from the sixties; he braked so hard that I hit my head against the windshield. Disappointed and alarmed I asked, 'Is this it?' This seemed to please Stein. With exaggerated movements he slithered over the icy concrete towards a woman in a house dress who had just stepped out of the front door. A pale, puny child clung to the house dress. I rolled down the car window, heard him call out with jovial warmth, 'Mrs Andersson!' – I had always hated the way he dealt with people of this type – saw how he offered her his hand and how she did not take it but dropped a huge bunch of keys into it. 'There's no water when it's freezing,' she said. 'Supply line's broken. But they're going to turn the electricity on next week.' The child hanging on to her house dress began to bawl. 'Doesn't matter,' Stein said, slithering back to the car, stopping at my rolled-down window to rotate his pelvis elegantly and obscenely. He said, 'Come on baby, let the good times roll.' I said, 'Stein, stop that.' I felt myself blushing. The child let go of the woman's dress and took an amazed step towards us.

'They used to live in it,' Stein said as he restarted the engine; he went in reverse back onto the road. The snow was falling more heavily now. I turned around and saw the woman and the child standing in the illuminated rectangle of the doorway until the house disappeared behind a curve. 'They're mad because they had to get out a year ago. It wasn't me who kicked them out, it was the owner from Dortmund. I only bought it. As far as I'm concerned they could have stayed on.' I said, uncomprehending, 'But they're disgusting,' and Stein said, 'What is disgusting?' and threw the bunch of keys into my lap. I counted the keys, there were twenty-three, really small ones and very large ones, all old and with beautifully curved handles. I sang under my breath, 'The key to the stable, the key to the attic, the one for the gate, for the barn, for the parlour, for the dairy, mailbox, cellar, garden gate,' and suddenly – without really wanting to – I understood Stein, his enthusiasm, his anticipation, his excitement. I said, 'It's nice that we're driving there together, Stein.' He refused to look at me and said, 'In any case, from the veranda you can see the sun going down behind the church tower. We'll be there soon. After Angermünde comes Canitz, and Canitz is where the house is.'

Canitz was worse than Lunow, worse than Templin, worse than Schönwalde. Grey, cowering houses on both sides of the curving country road, many windows boarded up, no store, no bakery, no inn. The snow flurries were getting heavier. 'A lot of snow here, Stein,' I said, and he replied, 'Of course,' as though he had bought the snow along with the house. When the village church appeared on the left side of the street, really beautiful and red with a round bell tower, Stein started to make an odd humming sound, like a fly bumping against closed windows in the summer. He drove into a small cross street, brought the car to a stop, and at the same time took his hands off the steering wheel with an emphatic gesture, saying, 'That's it.'

I looked out of the car window and thought, 'That's it for another five minutes.' The house looked as though it would cave in suddenly and soundlessly. I climbed out and shut the car door carefully as though the next jolt might be too much. Stein and I walked towards the house on tiptoe. The house was a ship. It sat at the edge of this Canitz village street like a proud vessel beached in times long gone by. It was a large, two-storey country manor house of red brick; its skeletonized gable roof had two wooden horses' heads, one at each end. Most of the windows had lost their glass panes, the crooked veranda was held together only by dense ivy, and cracks as wide as your thumb ran through the brickwork. The house was beautiful. It was *the* house. And it was a ruin.

The gate from which Stein was trying to remove a sign saying 'For Sale' collapsed with a plaintive sound. We climbed over it, then I stood still, startled by the expression on Stein's face. I saw him disappear behind the ivy on the veranda. Soon afterwards a window frame fell off the house, Stein's excited face appeared amidst the jagged glass of one pane, lit up by the light from a kerosene lamp.

'Stein!' I shouted. 'Get out of there! It's going to collapse!'
'Come in!' he yelled back. 'It's *my house*!'
I briefly asked myself why that should be reassuring, then

stumbled over garbage bags and trash onto the veranda. Its boards groaned, and the ivy immediately swallowed up all the light; in disgust I pushed the vines aside, then Stein's ice-cold hand pulled me into the hall. I grabbed it. I grabbed for his hand; suddenly I didn't want to lose his touch again, and especially not the glow of his wretched little kerosene lamp. Stein was humming. I followed him.

He pushed all the shutters out into the garden. We could see the last of the daylight through the red splinters of glass in the doors. The bunch of keys that felt heavy in my jacket pocket was totally unnecessary, as all the doors either stood open or were no longer there. Stein held up the lamp, pointed, described, stood breathless before me, wanted to say something, said nothing, pulled me along. He stroked the banisters and door handles, tapped on walls, picked at the wallpaper and marvelled at the dusty plaster underneath. He said, 'You see?' and, 'Feel this,' and, 'How do you like this?' I didn't have to answer; he was talking to himself. He knelt on the kitchen floor and wiped the filth off the tiles, muttering; I clung to him all this time, yet I no longer existed. On the walls, somebody had scrawled *I shot the moon tonight. I was here, Mattis. No risk, no fun.* I said, 'I shot the moon tonight,' Stein turned towards me, suddenly confused, and said, 'What?' I said, 'Nothing.' He grabbed my arm and pushed me along in front of him, kicking the back door out into the garden and dragging me down a few stairs. 'Here.'

I said, 'What do you mean – here?'

'Well, everything!' said Stein. I had never seen him so unrestrained and brash. 'A Brandenburg lake, chestnut trees in the yard, one and a half acres of land, you can plant your goddamn grass here, and mushrooms and hemp and shit. Plenty of room, you understand? Plenty of room. I'll build you a salon here, and a billiard room, and a smoking room, and separate rooms for everyone and a big table in back of the house for your shitty meals and crap, and then you can get up and walk over to the Oder and snort coke there till your skull splits.' He twisted my head roughly in the direction of the garden and the land beyond. It was too dark, and I could scarcely make out anything, I began to shiver.

I said, 'Stein. Please. Stop.'

He stopped. He was silent. We looked at each other, we were breathing hard and almost in the same rhythm. Slowly he put his hand on my face. I flinched, and he said, 'All right. All right, all right. Okay.'

I stood still. I didn't understand any of this, though remotely I did understand something but it was still much too far away. I was exhausted and weary. I thought of the others and felt a passing anger that they had left me here alone, that no one else was here to protect me from Stein, not Christiane, nor Anna, nor Heinze. Stein shuffled his feet and said, 'I'm sorry.'

I said, 'It doesn't matter. Never mind.'

He took my hand, his hand was warm now and soft, he said, 'So then, the sun behind the church tower.'

On the veranda he wiped the snow off the stair treads and invited me to sit down. I did. I felt incredibly cold. I took the lit cigarette he held out to me. I smoked, and stared at the church tower behind which the sun had already set. I had the guilty feeling that I should be saying something forward-looking, something optimistic. I felt confused. I said, 'In the summer, I'd take the ivy off the veranda. Otherwise we can't see anything if we want to sit here and drink wine.'

Stein said, 'Will do.'

I was sure he hadn't been listening at all. Sitting next to me he seemed tired. He looked out at the cold, empty, snowy street; I thought of summer, of that hour in Heinze's garden in Lunow, I wished that Stein would look at me once more the way he had looked at me then, and I hated myself for thinking it. I said, 'Stein, would you please tell me something? Could you please explain something to me?'

Stein flicked his cigarette into the snow and looked at me. 'What should I tell you? This, here, is one possibility, one of many. You can go with it, or you can forget it. I can go with it, or I can forget it and go somewhere else. We could do it together, or pretend that we never knew each other. It doesn't matter. I only wanted to show it to you, that's all.'

I said, 'You paid eighty thousand marks to show me one possibility, one of many? Did I understand that correctly? Stein? What's the point?'

Stein didn't react. He leaned forward and looked hard at the street, I followed his gaze; it was dim on the street, but the last light reflected by the snow made it hard to see. Someone was standing on the other side of the street. I squinted and sat up. The figure was about fifteen feet away, then it turned and walked into the shadows between two houses. A garden gate banged, I was convinced I had recognized the child from Angermünde, the pale, dumb child that had clung to the woman's house dress.

Stein got up and said, 'Let's go.'

I said, 'Stein – the child. From Angermünde. Why is it standing around here on the street, watching us?'

I knew he wouldn't answer. He held the car door open for me, I stood in front of him, waiting for something, for a touch, a gesture. I thought, 'But *you* always wanted to be with us.'

Stein said coolly, 'Thanks for coming with me.'

I got into the car.

*　　*　　*

I no longer remember what kind of music we listened to on the way back. In the weeks that followed I saw Stein only rarely. The lakes froze over, we bought ice skates, and at night we roamed through the woods and out over the ice carrying torches. We listened to Paolo Conte on Heinze's boombox, swallowed ecstasy, and read aloud the best parts from Bret Easton Ellis's *American Psycho*. Falk kissed Anna, and Anna kissed me, and I kissed Christiane. Sometimes Stein was there too. He kissed Henrietta, and whenever he did I looked away. We avoided each other. He hadn't told anybody that he had finally bought the house, nor did he tell them that he had driven out there with me. I didn't either. I didn't think about the house, but sometimes, when we threw our ice skates and torches into the trunk of his cab before driving back to the city I saw it contained roofing paper, wallpaper and paint.

In February Toddi fell through the ice on Lake Griebnitz. Heinze was skating wildly across the ice, holding up his torch and shouting, 'This is such fun, what a great time we're having, I can't believe it!' He was totally drunk, and Toddi was skating along behind him. We called out, 'Say, *Blue*, Toddi! Say it!' and then there was a crack, and Toddi disappeared.

We stood still. Heinze, his mouth open, skated a terrific loop, the ice hummed, wax dripped hissing from our torches. Falk sped off on his skates, tripping, Anna tore off her scarf, Christiane stupidly covered her face with her hands and screamed weakly. Falk crept along on his belly, Heinze was out of sight. Falk yelled for Toddi, and Toddi yelled back. Anna threw out her scarf, Henrietta clung to Falk's feet. I came to a stop. Stein also stopped. I took the lighted cigarette he held out to me. He said, 'Blue,' I said, 'Cold,' and then we began to laugh. We laughed, doubling over, and lay down on the ice, and the tears ran down our cheeks;

we laughed and couldn't stop, not even when they brought Toddi back, wet and shivering, and Henrietta said, 'Are you crazy or something?'

In March Stein disappeared. He didn't turn up for Heinze's thirtieth birthday, or for Christiane's premiere or Anna's concert either. He was gone, and when Henrietta, foolishly discreet, asked where he was, they shrugged their shoulders. I didn't shrug, but I didn't say anything. A week later his first postcard arrived. It was a photo of the village church in Canitz, and on the back it said:

The roof is waterproof. The child is blowing its nose, doesn't speak, is always here. The sun is dependable, I smoke when it's setting. I've planted something, you can eat it. I'll cut the ivy when you come. Remember, you still have the keys.

After that postcards came regularly. I waited for them; when they failed to come, I was disappointed. They always had photos of the church and always four or five sentences like little riddles, sometimes nice, sometimes incomprehensible. Stein often wrote – 'when you come'. He didn't write 'Come'. I decided to wait for 'Come' and then I would go there. In May there was no card, but instead a letter. I looked at Stein's clumsy, large handwriting on the envelope, crawled back into bed with Falk, and tore open the envelope. Falk was still asleep and snoring. Inside there was a newspaper clipping from the *Angermünder Anzeiger*. Stein had scribbled the date on the back. I pushed Falk's sleep-warmed body aside, unfolded the article, and read:

REGIONAL NEWS
Friday night the former manor house in Canitz burned down to its foundation. The owner, a Berliner who bought

*the eighteenth-century house six months ago and restored it,
has been reported missing since the fire. The cause of the fire
has not yet been established. So far the police are not ruling
out arson.*

I read it three times. Falk moved. I stared at the article, then
at Stein's handwriting on the envelope, then back again. The
postmark said Stralsund. Falk woke up and looked at me apa-
thetically for a moment, then reached for my wrist and, with the
nasty cunning of a fool, asked: 'What's that?'

I drew my hand away, climbed out of bed, and said, 'Nothing.'

I went to the kitchen and for ten minutes stood around stupidly
in front of the stove. The clock above the stove ticked. I ran
into the back room, pulled out the desk drawer and added
the envelope to the other cards and the bunch of keys. I
thought, 'Later.'

Camera Obscura

The artist is very short. Sometimes Marie wonders whether she's still in her right mind: the artist is much too short. She says to herself, You've lost your marbles, maybe because autumn is coming, or because the old restlessness is returning. The chill in her back, the rain?

The artist is really very short. At least three heads shorter than Marie. He is famous. Everybody knows him, at least everyone in Berlin does. He creates art with a computer and has written two books, and sometimes he talks on late-night radio shows. On top of that the artist is ugly. He has a very small proletarian head and is very dark: some people say he has Spanish blood. His mouth is incredibly small. Non-existent. His eyes, though, are beautiful, quite black and large; usually when he speaks he holds his hand in front of his face in such a way that you can see only those eyes. The artist's clothes are awful. He wears torn jeans – a child's size, Marie guesses – and always a green jacket, always sneakers. A black leather band is knotted around his left wrist. Some people say that regardless of all this the artist is incredibly intelligent.

Marie wants something from the artist. What it is she doesn't know. Perhaps the glamour of his fame. Perhaps to look even more beautiful beside an ugly person. Perhaps to penetrate and destroy his seeming impassiveness. Marie asks herself in all seriousness, whether she is still okay. Don't they look rather ridiculous together? Marie had always wanted to be only with beautiful people. It's weird to have to look down at a man. It's weird to imagine what it would be like if . . . Still, that's what Marie wants.

They kiss on the very first evening. Or rather, Marie kisses the artist. Suddenly he's standing in front of her, at this party, among all the Berlin celebrities, and Marie can't decide on which of the celebrities to cast her long, long gaze first. The artist offers himself. Suddenly he is standing in front of her with those beautiful black eyes, and Marie, having seen him on television, recognizes him immediately. He keeps pouring vodka into her glass and asks difficult questions. What does being happy mean to you? Have you ever betrayed someone? Do you feel bad if you've achieved something only because of your looks?

Marie drinks the vodka, hesitates, says: – Happiness is always the moment before. The second before the moment in which I actually ought to be happy. In that second I am happy and don't know it. I've betrayed a lot of people, I think. And I like achieving things because of my looks.

The artist stares at her. Marie stares back. She's good at that. The people around her are growing restless; the artist is really too short and too ugly. More out of spite than solidarity Marie bends down, takes the artist's head in both of her hands and kisses him on the mouth. He kisses her back, of course. Then Marie gives him her phone number and leaves, realizing only outside in the cold and clear night air how drunk she really is.

The artist waits three days, then calls her. Did he really – wait, that is? Marie assumes so. They spend an evening at a bar where Marie is freezing and has spells of weakness because the artist is constantly looking at her and doesn't want to talk. One morning they go for a walk in the park, the artist wearing stylish sunglasses that Marie likes. For one whole afternoon they sit in a café, and Marie tells him a little about herself. Otherwise she is silent. The artist says he doesn't like conversations on a meta-level.

Marie doesn't know what meta-level is supposed to mean. Whenever she goes to meet him she puts on the only pair of flat shoes she owns. The difference in their heights embarrasses her. It is autumn. Dying wasps tumble through the open window into Marie's room. She feels cold and wears gloves; the days are already short, and she is very often tired. Sometimes she tilts her head back and tries to laugh effervescently, but it doesn't come out right. One day the artist asks whether she would like to drive to the Baltic Sea with him for a couple of days sometime. Marie says yes and thinks of places like Ahlbeck, Fischland and Hiddensee, of a long white wintry beach, of shells and a calm sea. She does not think of the artist. She stands at her window, holding a cup of cold tea, and stares out into the street. She is confused nowadays, puts lighted cigarettes between her lips the wrong way round, leaves the water running, loses her keys. Once the artist calls her and actually says, I love you. Marie is squatting on the floor, the telephone receiver clamped between her head and shoulder, looking into the mirror. She closes her eyes slowly, and slowly opens them again. Now the artist isn't saying anything else, but she hears him breathing, softly, regularly, calmly. He is not nervous. Marie isn't either. Again she says, Yes, and is surprised that the answer comes so quickly. The artist hangs up.

When Marie thinks of his eyes she feels an ache in her back. His eyes are really beautiful. She is not *waiting* for him to call, she *knows* he will call. The artist seems to be quite content with his dwarfishness. He emphasizes it by moving in a fidgety and clownish way, walking like a tin soldier, sometimes doing a handstand in the middle of the street, making faces, doing magic tricks by putting coins into his ear and retrieving them from his nose. Since the kiss at the party he hasn't touched Marie. Nor she him. When they say goodbye he acts as though he's about to put his hand on her arm, but at the last moment he always draws it away again. He asks her, What does it mean when you look at me for such a long time? Marie answers, Closeness, aggression, also sexuality, and consent. She doesn't know whether that's true. The artist can't smile. When he thinks he's smiling, he's only squeezing his eyes together into narrow slits and pulling up the corners of his mouth. Marie doesn't find this convincing, and she tells him so, triumph in her voice. Could be, says the artist. For the first time he looks hurt.

In a café one evening, when Marie is already very drunk, she asks him whether he ever considered going to bed with her. She knows it's wrong, but she can't help herself, she's wanted to ask him for days. The artist says, I guess there have been women with whom I've made a greater effort. Marie is indignant, crosses her arms over her chest and decides not to say another word. The artist drinks his wine, smokes, looks at her, and says, You'd better leave now. Marie rides home on her bicycle, furious.

Later she phones him. I don't feel like being observed by you, says the artist: nevertheless he says he is willing to see her again. In a way he reminds Marie of an animal. A small animal. A black, hairy, creepy little monkey. She puts her low-heeled shoes into the closet, puts on high-heeled boots, and for the first time cycles to his apartment.

The artist opens the door but only after she has rung the bell three times. He's wearing his sneakers, torn jeans, his black sweater. He once told Marie that he always buys fifteen small-sized sweaters at a time and dyes them all black. It's warm in the apartment. Strangely neat and tidy. The walls are painted orange, with huge quantities of books, CDs, records. Would you like tea, the artist asks. Yes, says Marie sitting down at his desk – which isn't near the window but against the back wall – on the only chair in the room. Postcards, newspaper comic strips, photos, letters are pinned to the wall above the desk. Small pieces of paper layered on top of each other. The artist somewhere in the sunny South, a blond, puffy-cheeked child in his arms. Theatre programmes, a book review, neatly cut out. A strip of passport photos of the artist, shot from above because of his size, the flash creating a white spot on his forehead. A sentence in large letters on yellow paper: 'In times of betrayal landscapes are beautiful.' In the kitchen the artist is clattering around with the cups. Marie, biting her lower lip, is self-conscious and nervous. She hears his approaching steps rustle on the cork rug and turns around to face him, putting on a wooden smile. The artist sets the cups on the glass surface of the desk and asks, Music? Marie shrugs and clings to her cup. The artist puts a CD into the player. There is crackling in the loudspeakers, P.J. Harvey's voice is heard from very far away – *Is that all there is?* Depression music, Marie thinks, wondering whether she should say it out loud. The artist circles around her, looking very self-satisfied and sure of himself and observing her with a mocking expression. Marie clears her throat. The artist says, How about some computer? Marie replies, I don't know anything about that; the artist says amiably, That doesn't matter.

He switches on his computer. It hums softly, the black of the screen turning a bright clear blue. A smiling miniature computer appears and in the left margin of the screen various small icons open up. Marie twists her hands in her lap and feels very uncomfortable. The artist taps on the keys and circles around gently with the mouse; he pulls a fist-sized grey sphere out from behind the computer. In its centre is a gleaming black eye. He places the sphere in the middle of the desk and adjusts it so the black gleaming eye is focused directly on Marie's face. Marie stares at the sphere and the artist circles softly with the mouse. The screen turns white. Now, in its upper left corner, tiny light and dark grey squares appear, a grid of small dots spreading silently and quickly over the surface of the screen. The parting in Marie's hair, Marie's forehead, Marie's eyebrows, her eyes, her nose, mouth, chin, neck, the top of her breasts, an eerie black and white Marie-face.

That's hideous, Marie says. With a time delay and silently, the Marie-face on the screen repeats the words, That's hideous. It opens and closes its eyes and mouth, fishlike, horrible, dreadful. The image hasn't fully formed yet, the artist says. He keys in something, and the Marie-face becomes sharper, its contours clearer, and in the background the bookshelves on the right-hand wall of the room come into view, the window, the sky outside, grey on the screen, grey also in reality. You can shoot almost anything with it, the artist says, smiling unconvincingly and pleasantly at Marie. Marie smiles back, unconvinced. It is quiet. Marie endures the stare of the artist, who is no longer smiling. A third, black and beautiful eye has grown between his eyebrows. Marie blinks and the eye disappears again. The computer whirrs. Marie doesn't dare look at the screen, afraid of the grey and eerie Marie-face. The cork rug rustles because the artist is now coming towards her. Marie presses her back against the chair and stares fixedly into the artist's eyes, as though this might help keep the terror at bay. The artist puts his right hand on Marie's cheek: the hand is cool and soft. Marie briefly closes her eyes. Then his face is directly in front of hers, Marie stops breathing, and he kisses her on the lips. Marie is very sober. He probably is too. The kiss appears on the computer screen, with a time delay and silent, a grey repetition of an instant. Now Marie looks, past the face, past the closed eyes of the artist, at the screen on which his face snuggles up to hers, replacing her face: she opens her eyes, in black and white.

Something is turning in Marie's head. The artist takes a deep breath, presses against Marie, pushes his hand around to the back of her neck, down her back, inside her dress. Marie concentrates. Instead of seeing herself as usual from above, from a sort of bird's eye view, she looks at the screen, at this silent strange entwining of two human beings, and it is bizarre. It is warm in the room. Layered small pieces of paper hang above the desk, the artist somewhere in the sunny South, a blond, chubby-cheeked child in his arms. Too bad, Marie thinks, that you can see things for the first time only once.

The artist pulls Marie off the chair and onto the floor. At some point Marie is wearing nothing but her high-heeled boots, and then not even those. On the computer screen you see a wall of bookshelves, the back of an empty chair, a window, and outside, a darker sky.

This Side of the Oder

Koberling is standing on the hill as they arrive. The hill is a mound of soil that Koberling piled up with his own hands in the middle of the garden two years ago. Back then Constance had laughed and called it 'Field Marshal Hill'; he had countered with 'Napoleon Hill', and the name stuck. From there he has a view of the lawn, the veranda, the shady entrance to the kitchen, and the rolling meadows beyond which flows the Oder.

Koberling is standing on Napoleon Hill and smoking a cigarette; he shades his eyes with one hand and stares toward the horizon. Somewhere over there is the Oder, hidden in its riverbed. Somewhere over there, too, is Constance, taking her daily walk in the afternoon heat. The child is sleeping in the kitchen, exhausted by the summer. Koberling brushes away a wasp and thinks of autumn. The sound of a car's engine comes creeping up the sandy road like an illusion. Koberling turns his head, listening, and squints; no, no car ever comes driving up the sandy road except his own. It's not an illusion though. The sound of a diesel engine, a crunch of pebbles, Koberling beside himself, his heart pounding. Out of the corner of his right eye he catches sight of an old Mercedes. Koberling remains motionless, wants to be invisible, thinks, Keep on going. The Mercedes stops in front of the garden gate. Dust from the road swirls up, the door opens on the passenger side and Anna climbs out. Koberling recognizes her immediately. She looks the same as before, same as back then, only bigger, taller, a grown-up child. 'Koberling!' she shouts and stalks around the car in high-heeled shoes, stopping at the garden gate. She's wearing a red dress and is deeply tanned. The window on the driver's side is being rolled down and a young man with matted hair sticks his head out, yawning. Koberling has butterflies in his stomach and says very softly and viciously, 'Pothead.'

'Hey!' Anna shouts. 'We've just come back from Poland. We don't have any money left, and we thought we could stay with you, just for a few days. Koberling! Do you remember me?'

Koberling crushes the cigarette under his foot and comes down off the hill. 'I remember you. I can hear you. No need to shout like that.'

Anna's hand is on the handle of the garden gate, and the pothead is languidly peeling himself out of the car. Now Koberling can see that he's wearing unbelievably dirty jeans. Max calls from the kitchen in a sleepy and cracked child's voice, and Koberling knows that the light is falling on the little bed they've made for him on the window seat and that the flies are circling the lamp; suddenly he feels weak, overwhelmed. Where is Constance, he thinks, Constance who could be taking all this off my shoulders, because I don't want any visitors and especially no potheads.

He wipes the sweat from his upper lip and takes the pebbled path towards the garden gate. The crunch of the pebbles is surprisingly loud. Anna, Koberling thinks. Anna. You and your clown father, ridiculous buffoon, circus fool. When you were a child I once slapped you because you jumped on my back while I was meditating on the lawn in front of your house. When you were a child you didn't matter to me. I sat in the kitchen with your clown father and we talked and drank ourselves under the table. At worst you got on my nerves with your chocolate-smeared mouth, and you still get on my nerves now.

Koberling pushes back the bolt and pulls open the garden gate, smiling like an idiot, sweating incredibly. 'Wow, Koberling,' Anna says, grins, and follows this with a sort of 'Oh. Wow, Koberling. It must be years since the last time we saw each other. Years!'

'Yes,' Koberling says, 'Years.'

The pothead takes two lethargic steps toward Koberling, and extends a dirty hand. Koberling doesn't take it. He remains protectively near the gate as though this would make them understand, as though the mere presence of the silent and tense bastion of his body would make it clear to them that they should leave. That visitors were not welcome here. That old friendships no longer counted. But they do not understand. They stand there and stare. Koberling turns and takes the gravel path back to the veranda and, speaking into the blue, says, 'You can stay if you want to. There's a guest room in the attic.'

Toward evening Constance returns from her walk, no later than usual but for Koberling later than ever before. He's sitting on the veranda with Anna and the pothead, whose name he doesn't want to know, smoking one cigarette after the other. Max squats on the floor in front of the pothead, listening to his jumbled stories. Extraterrestrials, Druids, New Guinea, the end of the world. Max's mouth is wide open, a rope of spittle running down his chin, his left hand resting on one of the pothead's shoes: from time to time he tugs gently and absently at the shoelaces. Koberling resents Max's unprejudiced trust in this pothead. What an idiot, Koberling thinks. Max, this guy's what I'd call an idiot.

Anna sits cross-legged in a wicker chair, staring at Koberling, and lapses into childhood recollections. 'Something once happened with you, Koberling. Some funny business, I can't remember what exactly. I only know that you and my father were sitting at the kitchen table late into the night. Hey, Koberling, do you remember?'

Koberling makes no attempt to help her. He could haul out that business about the slap. He could tell her that as a child during those summers in the country she really was brown as a hazelnut. He could flatter her and remind her of all the silly children's jokes she used to tell, which her clown father proudly wrote down in an orange-coloured notebook. He could tell her that she used to be skinny and wiry, that she would disappear in the morning, taking the bridge across the river, into the woods, and not come back till evening, scratched all over, her legs covered with ticks. He could say, 'Your clown of a father left you alone. He allowed you to do whatever you wanted, so you'd simply disappear for the entire day. You weren't really there, not for any of us, and presumably that's your big childhood trauma today.'

But he doesn't feel like it. She doesn't interest him. Her clown father no longer interests him. He would like to sit here, in silence, undisturbed. Koberling lights another cigarette and realizes that he has been grinding his teeth all this time. Constance comes walking up the gravel path, a bounce in her step, dreadfully relaxed. Too late, Koberling thinks, too late my dear, for now they're here and they won't be leaving soon.

Constance recognizes Anna immediately. She smiles a beaming and convincing smile, claps her hands softly and briefly holds them up to her face. She laughs, and plants her hands on her hips. Koberling is disgusted. He can anticipate what she's about to say: 'Anna! Little skinny Anna, and at least fifteen years older now. I can't believe it's really you sitting here!' Anna beams, looking embarrassed. She introduces the pothead, then looks over at Koberling, shy. Koberling suddenly pushes back his chair and flees into the kitchen. Little skinny Anna. What nonsense. He takes olives, cheese, salami, out of the refrigerator. Cut the bread, uncork the wine, the same as back then, the same as always. Now we'll eat supper, Koberling thinks. Now we'll eat, now we'll do something, even if it's only eating the goddamn food.

*   *   *

Darkness comes early because it's almost autumn. Under the plum trees at the back of the garden the light is already grey; the Oder will be pink and light blue by now. Koberling thinks it's taken him forty-seven years to find out that the wheat fields and the lakes and rivers become light again just before night falls. He needed this house to find that out. Maybe also Max, and Constance, too. If things were normal the child would already be sleeping, snoring softly, his cheeks red. He himself would be sitting on the veranda with Constance, reading or not talking. At some point he would sit down at his computer and type two or three sentences of dialogue for one of the screenplays he writes for a living. Two or three short and strange sentences, like every other evening. The light of the desk lamp would be green, because green is calming. The moths would tumble against the window screen, and he would find it both good and shitty living like this.

Now, though, the pothead is standing on Napoleon Hill rolling himself a joint. What a jerk. His absurd Zippo lighter flares up, and Koberling can smell the sweetish hashish. He thinks of Rose Martenstein. Rose Martenstein who came to a carnival party dressed as the Queen of the Night and collapsed unconscious on the kitchen floor after eating a hashish cookie, a doll in black satin. Sure, he had smoked hashish too. With Anna's clown father, for one. They'd be sitting in the garden, smoking one joint after another, and Anna's clown father would shout, 'Swazi grass!' and, 'Off to Swaziland!' till Koberling fell off his chair, laughing. Anna would be sleeping in her room under mosquito netting, talking in her sleep, and Koberling didn't know that twelve years later his own round-headed child Max would be born. How should he have known? How could he have? Back then he didn't even want to acknowledge Anna.

The pothead on top of Napoleon Hill turns around and motions to Koberling with his joint. Koberling gestures back an exaggerated refusal, and the pothead shrugs and ambles down off the hill. The glowing end of his joint disappears between the plum trees, and Koberling lingers irresolutely near the kitchen door. Constance and Anna are still sitting on the veranda, Max on Constance's lap, thumb in mouth. The child hasn't said a word to Koberling in the last four hours. He has clung to Anna or the pothead by turns, behaving as though he'd never seen another human being other than his mother and Koberling. Koberling thinks that's wrong. Max ought to be hiding behind him, ought to be asking him whether these guests are okay or not.

Anna talks about Poland. Max stares at her and from time to time breathes deeply, in and out. 'I can't understand why you still haven't been there when it's so close. They have storks there the way Berlin has pigeons. The Poles were mowing the fields, and sixty or seventy storks were walking in the furrows behind the tractors, looking for insects. And you wouldn't believe what ice-cream eaters the Poles are. *Lody* and *lody*, wherever you look they're constantly eating ice-cream.'

Max takes his thumb out of his mouth and says very clearly, 'Ice-cream.' Koberling feels tenderness creeping up his back. What a weird conversation. And the child picks out the one word he knows – ice-cream.

Anna talks, gestures with her hands, is constantly tucking her hair behind her ears. 'Constance. How are you doing here?'

Constance's voice, very deep and a little husky. Doing well. It's lonely. Koberling doesn't want a lot of visitors, a retreat after all those years in the city, a summer retreat; anyway in the autumn it's back to Berlin. Long days. Hot days. Koberling spending a lot of time at his desk – a lie – and she herself going on walks through the Oderbruch, the Oder marshes, a most beautiful bit of nature. Good for the child too. Children belong in the country. Max is happy, she is too. And Koberling? He has trouble with being happy, but still . . .

Constance's hand, always arranging things. Constance, the perpetual organizer. Four, five sentences, a life forged in one casting, one stroke of the pen and no more questions. It's that simple. In the shade by the kitchen door Koberling closes his eyes and opens them again. Anna has stopped talking. Now, in the total darkness, a sudden indignant croaking of frogs. A brief moment. Anna lights a cigarette and says, 'Yes,' begins again to tell her Poland stories, the ice-cream stories, her voice sounding somewhat remote, disconcerted. In the dark Koberling senses Constance's smile. He is surprised at how calmly she sits there listening to Anna's stories. In fact he is surprised at the interest she's showing in these guests, the obvious pleasure she takes in their visit. It doesn't matter who comes, Koberling thinks. It just doesn't matter. Anyone could be sitting here and she'd listen the same way, eagerly, glad to have a break from me for a while. It's because we've been here by ourselves the entire summer. But that's what we had agreed to do. We wanted to be by ourselves. I wanted to be alone.

Koberling goes back into the kitchen, turns out the light and sits down on Max's little day bed by the window. The contours in the garden have become sharper. Anna's red dress is dark, appears black. Koberling looks at her and feels nothing. She is young, has her father's clown face, everything round, round eyes, round mouth. A gap between her teeth that's going to make her look common ten years from now. Brown hair, very brown skin.

She's probably taking classes at the university, Koberling thinks. Journalism, and a foreign language. The pothead probably tends bar in some trendy hangout and apart from that squanders his days. In the summertime they load their friends into old cars, drive to the Brandenburg lakes, guzzle wine till they pass out, and are convinced that the things that happen to them don't happen to anyone else. Idiotic. All of it idiotic. He rubs his eyes and feels tired. The days when he used to ask everyone, 'What do you think?' and 'What do you do?' are over. Koberling can't imagine that he ever asked these questions. Disgusting, almost embarrassing, recollections of sitting around in bars all night, of swapping ideals, the destruction of illusions, carefully tended common interests. Hypocrisy, all of it, Koberling thinks. Anna's clown father was always just waiting for me to stop speaking so that he could begin with his utopias, his crazy head-in-the-clouds realities. And the same with me. I argued with him, I just wanted to out-talk him, when actually we both should have kept our mouths shut.

Max slides off Constance's lap, walks across the veranda and stands at the kitchen door. 'Why d'you sit there in the dark?' His voice is a little hoarse.

'Darkness is the friend of thieves,' Koberling says. 'Come on. Time for bed, time for the sand dragon and all that stuff.' He stands and lifts Max up: the child smells of summer and country-road dirt. 'Promise me,' Koberling feels like saying to him, 'promise me that . . .' But he doesn't say it.

'Are you two going to bed?' Constance asks from the veranda, her wicker chair creaking as she gets up.

'Yes,' Koberling replies, hurrying to the stairs, 'we're going to bed.' In his arms Max is already asleep. Anna calls out, 'Goodnight, Koberling!'

When he wakes up the next morning she is standing at the foot of his bed, smiling, her head cocked to one side, like a bird's. Glittering sunlight streams in through the window, and a fly bumps against the panes of glass. Koberling squints in the bright light and gropes under the covers for Constance, who is no longer lying beside him. No dreams, he thinks with relief. I didn't dream, not about her clown father nor about the past, not about smoking grass nor about sex.

Anna is shaking the bedstead so hard it sets her hair flying. 'Koberling! You sleepyhead! It's already noon, the others all drove to the city, and breakfast is ready. You're supposed to get up and show me the Oderbruch!'

'Says who?' Koberling asks. He is suddenly furious, sleep in his eyes and a bad taste in his mouth. That Anna should have dared to come in here, bursting into the intimacy of his bedroom like a child. She probably sneaked through the house first, looking into chests and drawers with her naïve curiosity. Koberling sits up and pulls the covers over his chest. 'Out,' he says, 'get out now. I want to get up by myself. I want to be left in peace.'

Anna lets go of the bedstead, still smiling, and walks toward the door. 'I'll be in the garden, in case you want to know.' Koberling doesn't want to know and doesn't answer. He waits until he hears her footsteps downstairs in the kitchen and closes his eyes again. Lying there. Just lying there, in a state of exhaustion, on a seesaw between waking and dreaming. He has never felt refreshed and rested in the morning after eight hours of sleep. Always exhausted. Before, at night in his one-room apartment, Berlin and winter, he used to go to sleep dreading all the days, months, years that still awaited him. Time. Time that had to be filled up, conquered, annihilated. Then Constance came. A shared two-room apartment, Berlin and winter. In his memory always winter, warmth under the quilt, the commitment to Constance that was connected with a feeling of capitulation. Constance, behind whom Koberling hid and never emerged. Refuge and acquiescence. They used to fall asleep next to each other, saying, 'Fly slowly.' Time retreated, his dread crouched in the farthest recess of his mind. Then finally Lunow, this house, the breathing of the child, time completely dissolving. And then, again the dread – even greater than ever before – some nights when a car drove by and projected the circling shadow of the venetian blinds on the ceiling of their room. Perhaps because of this his exhaustion. Because sleep has to overcome dread, always.

Finished, Koberling thinks. Finished and done. It can't be that two little people from Berlin can walk in here and get me all mixed up. Mixed up about what? He gets up and opens the window. The fly moves out into the open in a straight line and is gone. Outside, the sky, a vast blue vault, and a newly woven spider web trembling in the window frame.

In the kitchen there's coffee on the table and an egg tucked into its woollen cosy. Constance has left him a note. *Dear Koberling, went shopping with Max and Tom, back sometime in the afternoon, why don't you show Anna the Oderbruch, hugs and kisses.*

Show Anna the Oderbruch. An imposition. Koberling looks at the little beelike squiggle that Max has put under Constance's large flowing script and places his hand on his stomach. He rolls the egg undecidedly across the wooden table top, pours coffee into a mug and sits down on the veranda. Anna, barefoot, is in the orchard picking raspberries. The noonday heat is oppressive and close, and Koberling already longs for the evening. The coffee is lukewarm and tastes bitter, leaving a furry taste on his tongue. Koberling pours it over the veranda railing into the flowerbed and says softly, 'For Janis.'

Anna looks at him and picks up the berry bowl, then comes up onto the veranda. 'What did you say?'

Koberling doesn't look up but gazes into his empty coffee cup and says, 'For Janis. Your father always used to say that, long ago, when he poured leftover wine into the garden, "For Janis, for Janis Joplin."'

'Yes,' Anna says simply.

Koberling doesn't dare look up. Suddenly he feels terribly embarrassed about something. He stares at Anna's feet, at her dirty little toes.

She hides her left foot behind the right. Says, 'I thought I'd stay behind. Otherwise you would have woken up and found us all gone.'

Koberling looks up now, and acts preoccupied. Anna tilts her head and smiles at him, unsure. 'Wasn't it okay to wake you?'

What can one say to that? Nothing. And Anna doesn't seem to expect an answer. She sits down next to him, lights a cigarette, and inhales deeply. 'Tom likes it here. I do too. It's so peaceful, and besides we are having an Indian summer.'

Koberling makes a sound that could be interpreted as agreement or disapproval. Anna stares at him sideways. Koberling becomes restless and turns the empty cup in his hands; he can feel that Anna is slowly tensing up.

'Do you want to show me the Oderbruch or don't you? I mean, do you feel like going for a walk with me, or would you rather keep on sitting here?' With the last words her voice gets louder, almost stern.

Cry a little, Koberling thinks. Cry a little because you don't know how to deal with me, and also because I remind you of the time I slapped you. He too lights a cigarette, then gets up, and says, 'Yes, well. We can go for a little walk if you want.'

As Koberling closes the garden gate behind him he feels he's in unsafe territory. The house, the garden, the veranda, and above all Napoleon Hill are no longer protecting him. His back against the wall. Anna stands in the road, shifting from one foot to the other and looking almost the way she did long ago, like the child from back then, across the bridge over the river, into the woods, and away.

Koberling marches off resolutely, Anna hurries along beside him, dust whirling up between their feet. The country road becomes narrower. At the foot of the hills it becomes a small path that winds upward, through fruit trees, up into the green. Koberling, hands in his pockets, stares straight ahead. He feels a tension in his back and is already grinding his teeth again. Anna aside. Even without Anna, he has never liked the walks into the Oderbruch. Constance does. Ever since Lunow has been there for her, Constance walks off every afternoon with a happy face and comes back with an even happier face. 'The hills, Koberling. Sometimes I think it's the hills. I find them calming.'

Koberling finds the hills disturbing. For him it's all too beautiful, too enchanted, a Tarkovsky landscape, almost sinister. Once last summer he went into the Oderbruch by himself. In a tree on one of the more distant hills – he could already see the Oder – hung a piece of meat. A big piece of meat, almost the size of a man – a cow or a pig – skinned, bloody, putrid, flies buzzing around it. Koberling, panting up hill, ready to see the Oder, to savour it, stopped and felt his heart lurch. The meat hung from one of the upper branches, the rope by which it was attached creaking and twisting. It looked like a vision, like a nightmare image, a monstrous and incomprehensible message, and Koberling turned, ran back down the hill, and screamed. Later Constance, sitting in the wicker chair on the veranda and smelling of violets, laughed and said, 'Don't be silly, Koberling. You only dreamed it.'

The next day, when they went to the Oderbruch together, the piece of meat had disappeared. Nothing was there any more. No rope, no flies, no message. They never talked about it again.

Anna kicks little pebbles, is smiling again, and whistles through the gap in her teeth. 'You don't want to talk, do you?'

'No,' Koberling says, 'I don't want to talk.' Says to himself, Talk about what, and peers through the fruit trees, straining to see. There is no vision. Nothing that he would see but Anna would not.

'That's all right,' Anna says. 'I don't want to talk either. Often I don't.' Koberling looks at her in ironic surprise, but she ignores him.

The last tall stalks of wheat still stand along the edge of the path. The trees have yellow edges, and a swarm of birds forms a triangle in the sky. In the distance the Oder gleams, a blue ribbon perforated by green river islands. The air above the meadows shimmers. Anna is breathing heavily. She twists her hair into a bun at the back of her neck.

Koberling remembers the beginning of a poem, *On the far side of the Oder, where the plain so wide*, or something like that, one of the countless poems that he used to recite to Anna's clown father on those lunatic walks at night on the moors. 'Listen to this one, and this one,' a helpless recital, a gush of words. Koberling walks along behind Anna, and his inability to describe, to express why the words sound so heart-wrenching – *On the far side of the Oder, where the plain so wide* – leaves him breathless. 'I understand,' Anna's father had said, again and again. 'I do understand.' But he couldn't have understood because Koberling himself didn't comprehend anything. He would like to grab Anna by the hair now, to shake her and slap her for the years of self-deception, for the years themselves. He wants to slap her again, to repeat himself. The Oder is dazzling, and the flat fields flow together into a green sea. Koberling calls her name and hears his voice, but as if coming from a great distance. Anna turns around, her red dress swinging into a wave. Koberling closes his eyes and thinks he is falling.

'Koberling? Are you all right?'

'Yes,' Koberling says. 'Everything's fine. I just want to go back now.'

Shortly before they reach Lunow – they can already see the country road, and behind the bend the house is about to appear – Anna touches his arm. Koberling takes a deep breath. The Oder is behind him, behind the hills, the distant unease already nearly forgotten. This will be the last time that he surrenders to it. Koberling quickens his pace. He would like to walk fast, to run, perhaps even to sing. An enormous relief spreads through him.

Anna stops and says, 'Koberling, I'd really like to know what there was between my father and you. I mean, I'd like to know why you no longer see each other, why you broke off the relationship.'

Koberling also stops and looks at her. She is smiling and looks hurt. 'There's no reason. There's no story there.' Koberling is surprised he even answered her. 'We had a few really good years together, then we saw each other less and less frequently, and at some point not at all anymore. Maybe it was because he had women I didn't like. And you got older, later on he spent a lot of time taking care of you. There were minor arguments we didn't clear up, some disagreements. We lived different lives, I think. That's all. No tragedies, nothing decisive.'

Anna turns around and takes the path through the meadow down to the road. She walks very quickly. Koberling follows her and would like to call out, 'Life isn't theatre, Anna!' He doesn't know whether she can still hear him. She is running.

That evening Koberling is sitting on the veranda with Constance. Anna has gone back to the Oderbruch with the pothead. They had eaten supper together, and Koberling had three glasses of wine. He feels the alcohol in his knees and in his stomach. A cloud of mosquitoes hangs over the plum trees, and Constance is blowing smoke rings into space.

'I hope that Max will never do that. I'm not just hoping he won't, I simply won't have it,' Koberling says, not looking at Constance but at the plum trees, out into the darkness of the garden.

'What?' says Constance sleepily. 'What ... will never do what?'

'What Anna did here,' says Koberling and hears a note of spite in his voice that he can't help. 'What she did by turning up here unexpectedly and under false pretences. When he grows up I don't want Max to turn up at Anna's father's place with some floozy on his arm and say – Hey, clown father!' Koberling raises his voice and mimics Anna. 'Hey, clown father, can we stay with you a couple of days? Only a couple of days, nothing special, just hang out, and at some point or other you can tell me why you stopped being friends with my father back then.'

Constance laughs and forms a big smoke ring with her lips. It glides away and dissolves. 'You're crazy, Koberling. Max doesn't even know Anna's father. And you probably aren't going to tell him anything either. And by the time Max grows up Anna's father may no longer be around.'

Next morning Constance and Max are singing along with the radio in the kitchen. Koberling is awakened by their voices, which mix in with that of the radio announcer. The sun is streaming through the window. No Anna in the room, no dreams during the night.

A summer day, Koberling thinks, picture perfect. He rumbles down the stairs, and pulls open the kitchen door. Max is sitting at the table, his mouth smeared with egg, looking blissful. Constance stands at the stove, her face a dark shadow against the sunlight. She doesn't look up, sings along with the radio, says, 'Good morning, Koberling.'

'Yes,' Koberling says, looking out into the garden, to the veranda, towards Napoleon Hill. Then says much too quickly, 'Where are they?'

The kettle begins to whistle. Constance turns off the gas and says, 'They left already. Anna wanted to go to some lake or other before it got really hot.'

Koberling goes over to the radio and turns it off. It becomes quiet in the kitchen. 'What? I don't understand. Why did they leave so soon?'

Constance pours hot water into the coffee filter, her expression strained, 'They didn't want to wake you again, Koberling. To abuse your hospitality. They left their address in Berlin and said they'd be happy if we visited them in the autumn.'

Koberling stares at Max. Max stares back and lets his egg spoon sink slowly onto the table. Koberling feels an ache in his stomach, like a tremendous insult. He opens the door to the veranda and pokes his left hand through a spider web between the doorposts. Indian summer. He says, 'By the time we go back to Berlin in the fall I'm sure they won't be together anymore,' the only pathetic put-down he can think of. Constance doesn't answer.

Acknowledgements

The author would like to thank the Autorenwerkstatt Prosa (Prose Writers' Workshop) of the Literarische Colloquium Berlin, the Kulturfond, the Akademie der Künste, the Alfred Döblin Haus in Wewelsfleth and especially Katja Lange-Müller, Burkhard Spinnen and Monika Maron for their support during her work on this book.

Penelope Fitzgerald

The Means of Escape

'Ten masterpieces, polished and perfect, and with such mesmerising characters that each story is equal to any novel.'

POLLY SAMSON, *Independent 'Books of the Year'*

'A remote Auckland farmhouse, an unvisited property rejected by the National Trust, a rain-soaked Brittany port – from the most unpromising of situations, Fitzgerald creates moments of high comedy, little pockets of slapstick in the midst of larger, more pregnant dramas. A superb collection.'

ALEX CLARK, *Guardian*

'So readable, so sharply tender'

ADAM MARS-JONES, *Observer*

'Of all the novelists in English of the last quarter-century, she has the most unarguable claim on greatness. *The Means of Escape* sets the seal on a career we, as readers, can only count ourselves lucky to have lived through.'

PHILIP HENSHER, *Spectator*

The Means of Escape was chosen as 'Book of the Year' by the following reviewers: Alex Clark (*Guardian*), David Sexton (*Evening Standard*), Jane Gardam (*Spectator*), Humphrey Carpenter (*Sunday Times*), John Murray-Browne (*Financial Times*), Polly Samson (*Independent*), Adam Mars-Jones (*Observer*), Hermione Lee (*Guardian*), Simon Brett (*Daily Mail*) and Julian Barnes (*Observer*).

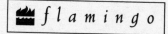

Jhumpa Lahiri

Interpreter of Maladies

Winner of the Pulitzer Prize 2000
Winner of the PEN/Hemingway Award
Winner of the NEW YORKER Prize for Best First Book

Jhumpa Lahiri's elegant stories tell the lives of Indians in exile, of people navigating between the strict traditions they've inherited and the baffling new world they must encounter every day. Whether set in Boston or Bengal, these sublimely understated stories, spiced with humour and subtle detail, speak with eloquence to anyone who has ever felt the yearnings of exile or the emotional confusion of the outsider.

'Jhumpa Lahiri is the kind of writer who makes you want to grab the next person you see and say "Read this!" She's a dazzling storyteller with a distinctive voice, an eye for nuance, an ear for irony. She is one of the finest short story writers I've read.'
AMY TAN

'Another side of India emerges when Lahiri sets her stories solely in Calcutta – where her protaganists are not Harvard academics but stair sweepers and outcasts. The nostalgic mist of homesickness lifted, India emerges raw, chaotic and often harsh . . . After reading three of these stories, I found myself rationing the remaining six, to try to make the book last longer. A lovely collection.' VICTORIA MILLER, *Scotsman*

flamingo

Marcel Möring

In Babylon

(translated from the Dutch by Stacey Knecht)

'Marcel Möring is beyond doubt one of the most imaginative
and perceptive novelists writing today.'

PAUL BINDING, *TLS*

The worst blizzard the East Netherlands has seen in many
years has left Nathan Hollander and his niece, Nina, snow-
bound in the deserted house of their late Uncle Herman.
Waiting for the storm to subside, they piece together the story
of their forefathers, a family of itinerant clockmakers who
came from Eastern Europe to the Netherlands in the seven-
teenth century and fled to America in 1939.

In this funny, quirky epic novel, Marcel Möring weaves a
gloriously inventive and very human story about man's
constant drive towards progression and expansion, his
coming and going, from the Old World to the New – and his
desire, despite everything, for home and homeland.

'Certain books make the reader recall what extraordinary
contraptions these objects are. Paper, some glue, ink: lo and
behold, a Tardis. Not much to look at from the outside, but
inside, infinite, forever unfolding, a tower to the clouds and a
tunnel deep into the earth, an arrow into the heart. *In Babylon*
is such a book. It is impossible to put this fat, rich novel into
any kind of category. It moves confidently between family
history, fairy story, love story, ghost story. Like the Jewish
family whose stories it unfolds, it is wide-ranging, adaptable,
learned and clever.'

ERICA WAGNER, *The Times*

 *flamingo*

Agnès Desarthe

Five Photos of My Wife

'A subtle and sly dissection of love, loss and truth . . . Full of charm and imagination, and darkly funny, too.'   *Elle*

Still reeling from the death of his beloved wife Telma, old Max Opass writes to his daughter with news of his empty days and humdrum activities – and tells her that he's decided to have Telma's likeness committed to canvas. To start with, he looks up 'Artists' in the Yellow Pages, picks a few at random, and commissions each to produce a portrait of his wife, working from five snapshot photographs for reference. But while one artist intimidates Max, another prompts him to pity; a pair of art students baffle him; and a bridge-playing acquaintance turns out to have the elderly hots for him. And with each subsequent moving, sometimes comic encounter, the reader comes to realize that Max's grasp on who his wife really was perhaps is not so sure after all . . .

'A rare tribute to the love of a wife . . . Desarthe's gentle novel, lucidly translated by Adriana Hunter, is the kind of mood piece at which the French excel. While many kinds of art are evoked (acrylic, oils, collage and video), her own prose suggests a watercolour – delicate, subtle and full of charm.'
MICHAEL ARDITTI, *Daily Mail*

'Well told, elegantly conceived and constructed'
DOMINIC BRADBURY, *The Times*

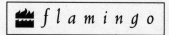 *flamingo*